Ceri,

Thank y
review on

I hope you enjoy it.
Regards, Milo

A SURPRISE PARTY

AND FOUR OTHER STORIES

A SURPRISE PARTY

AND FOUR OTHER STORIES

Milo McGivern

WITH ILLUSTRATIONS BY Yuliya Somina

Matador
9 Priory Business Park,
Wistow Road, Kibworth Beauchamp,
Leicestershire LE8 0RX
Tel: 0116 279 2299
Email: books@troubador.co.uk
Web: www.troubador.co.uk/matador
Twitter: @matadorbooks

ISBN 978 1800464 711

British Library Cataloguing in Publication Data.
A catalogue record for this book is available from the British Library.

Printed and bound by CPI Group (UK) Ltd, Croydon, CR0 4YY
Typeset in 12pt Minion Pro by Troubador Publishing Ltd, Leicester, UK

To Mum and Dad – for all the opportunities you created for me, and for your constant love and education.

And to Surbiton Hockey Club, where I spent many happy years standing on pitches on cold, dark winter afternoons.

TALES

HOW TO FIND THE LOCATION OF THE ISLAND OF ANIMAUX

Using Google Maps type the island location, included at the start of each story, into the search field (for example, 13N 90W – remember to put a space between the two coordinates). When you click the search button you will be taken to the relevant place on the map. Zoom out until you can see what part of the world Animaux is close to. In this case, off El Salvador. But be quick, as the island is moving all the time!

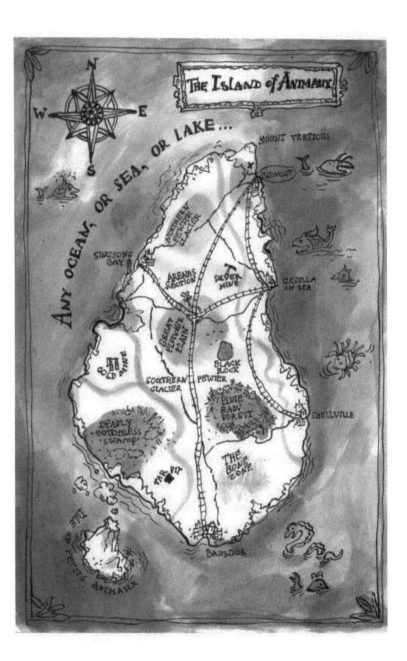

ONE

A SURPRISE PARTY

Island of Animaux location:

» latitude 1° south

» longitude 33° east

SCENE ONE – RED LETTER DAY

"Today's the day!" gobbled Aubrey happily as he looked at the calendar that was nailed to the kitchen wall.

He had put a big red circle around today's date seven days before, when Wincot had triumphed over Brusdor in the Animaux Cup Final. Since then, Aubrey had been getting more and more excited as the special day drew closer.

And now it had arrived, there was so much to do. Where should he start? Should he tidy the front room? Should he do the shopping? Should he cut the grass? Should he preen himself in front of the bathroom mirror? Should he sit in his armchair, with a silly look on his face and staring into space? Yes, the last one seemed like a very good idea, so he decided to do that straight away.

Aubrey walked from the kitchen to the front room. As he settled into his armchair, assuming the funny look, Clifford came down the stairs.

"G'day, Aubs, how's life?"

"Just wonderful – couldn't be better," said Aubrey with a jolly tone, continuing to stare at nothing in particular with the funny expression still on his face.

"What's wrong, Aubs?" asked Clifford, looking at him with concern. "Have you got a problem with your eyes? Do you need to go to the optician, or something?"

"The optician? No, my eyesight is fine. Why do you ask?" replied the turkey.

"I thought you had developed a squint, mate. I wished you good morning just now and you didn't look at me when you answered. There could be a number of reasons. First, you were being a little bit rude. That's probably the likeliest reason. Second, you have been sleep-walking and are still in a trance. That's an interesting possibility, although perhaps the most far-fetched. Third, during the night your eyeballs rotated in their sockets and you can now see sideways. That's the daftest possibility, but I think it's also the funniest. And so that's why I asked about the optician."

Aubrey turned and faced the platypus. "Clifford, sometimes you think too much. Your imagination runs away with you and you end up saying strange things. Your comment about my eyeballs rotating was particularly unpleasant."

"Point taken, Aubs. But can I ask why you were staring out of the window? What were you thinking about?"

"I was thinking about what I have to do first," Aubrey said vaguely.

"You've lost me, Aubs," said Clifford, scratching his head with his flipper. "I'm not following you at all."

"What I need to do first for my surprise party," replied Aubrey.

"Party? Are you going to have a party?"

"Yes. Later today. It's to celebrate us winning the cup last week. Oh, Clifford, don't you remember?"

"Of course I remember winning the cup. That was a great afternoon. But it's the first time you've mentioned a party," said Clifford. "But no worries. I love parties. Ripper! What time is it due to start?"

"Two o'clock this afternoon. But time is marching on, my friend from Down Under. There's lots to do, so we can't afford to lose another moment."

Just then Walli came out from the cupboard under the stairs. She had been in there since 6am, having got up much earlier than Aubrey or Clifford. Walli had been having a wonderful time, snuffling and snorting in all the dust and the cobwebs. She'd also found a strange grape-sized, squashy oval of black stuff in one of the corners. Walli wasn't sure what it was but had a quick lick before losing interest, noticing that it had a waxy and slightly sour taste.

"Howzit, have I missed something?" she asked her two friends.

"Aubs is going to have a party," quackled Clifford.

"Ooooh, lovely," squealed Walli. "I haven't been to a party for ages. What's the theme?"

"Theme? What do you mean?" said Aubrey. He was not an expert at throwing parties, and was therefore unfamiliar with Walli's language.

"Well, will there be dressing-up? Do your guests need to come in fancy dress or special clothes?"

"No, it's not that kind of party," replied Aubrey, feeling more confident that he could understand the warthog better. "It's a surprise party."

"Oooooohhhhh, smashing! I love surprise parties. They're the best kind. Hogtastic! Who will be coming?" asked Walli, jumping up and down with excitement.

"Ah, you'll have to wait and see," said Aubrey. "It's a surprise!"

Ever the organiser, Clifford thought it was time to get the party show on the road. "Right, let's get started on the preparations," he said. "What are your plans, Aubs?"

"Well, I'm going to town," Aubrey began. "I'll get the food and drink from Maureen Moose's Mini Mart – hopefully she'll give me credit as I'm a little short of money at the moment. And I'll get the decorations from Vicky Vulture's Party Shop – again hopefully on credit. You two wait here and you can help me with everything when I get back."

"No need for you to rush to town, Aubs. We can do everything ourselves," said Clifford.

"What do you mean?" asked Aubrey, surprised.

"Back in Oz, when platypuses have parties we make all the food and drink and decorations ourselves. You could say that we're experts at parties. So we have a wonderful time and it doesn't cost us anything."

"I'm not sure that's a very good idea," said Aubrey, looking worried. "I want my party to go really well and for creatures to remember it for a long time. Hopefully they will, then perhaps they'll invite me to their parties."

"Of course it's a good idea. All you need to do is use your imagination. Trust me, mate," said Clifford, his brown eyes twinkling. He clapped his front flippers briskly. "Right – we need to get our act together. Walli, you're on food. Aubs, you do the drinks. I'm on games. Let's go!"

"But I still don't know how we're going to do this," said Aubrey.

"Look, mate. You're holding things up. Just make things out of anything you find. Be creative. Go on – free your inner self. You'll be fine."

"OK," said Aubrey, still clueless about what was required. "I'll try my best."

SCENE TWO – GREAT IDEAS, GHASTLY DELIVERY

With that the friends all rushed off in different directions then, changing their minds, all rushed back in the direction they'd started from, almost knocking each other over. But then they got on

with things. Finally, after a great deal of squabbling and gobbling, skulking and sulking, quackling and squealing, but also some very hard work mixed with lots of imagination, they all said they had finished.

They gathered in the kitchen. Clifford decided he wanted to be in charge of seeing how they had all got on. "Right," he said. "Aubs, let's start with you. What drinks did you make?"

"I made three types. The first is my old favourite, snail smoothie." Aubrey pointed towards a large jug of grey liquid standing on the kitchen table. "You need to watch out for the bits of shell in it. And the slime."

Clifford and Walli looked apprehensively at the jug, both secretly deciding that they wouldn't take the first drink.

Aubrey then gestured towards a wooden box, also on the table. "Second, there's sawdust squash. That's rather dry and difficult to pour. And even more difficult to swallow. Normally you should have it with a slice of lemon. But we don't have a lemon, so you'll just have to pretend."

Clifford and Walli looked at each other. Did Aubrey have any idea how to make party drinks?

But Aubrey hadn't finished. "And last but not least, there's stinging nettle fizz. I'm rather proud of that one. Would you like to try any of them?"

Walli gave Clifford a gentle nudge, indicating that she wasn't feeling thirsty – at least not for the drinks Aubrey had 'created'.

"All right, mate," said Clifford, suspecting he wasn't going to enjoy the next few moments. "I'll try the stinging nettle fizz. That sounds weird."

Aubrey picked up an old saucepan that was lying in the middle of the kitchen floor and poured some of the contents into a glass. The fizz was dark green, very thick, and seemed to be a little bit lumpy.

Aubrey handed the glass to Clifford. "Tell me what you think," he said. "I made the recipe up, but I think it's come out rather well."

Clifford looked suspiciously at the glass and sniffed it. "It's got a rather an odd smell," he said. "I have never smelt a stinging nettle before, but this doesn't smell like I imagined it would. I was expecting the scent of grass or perhaps leaves. Oh well, here goes." With that, Clifford took a big swig of the fizz, swirled it around inside his bill for a few seconds, then gulped it down.

He coughed once, hiccupped twice, then let out the most enormous foul-smelling burp. "Interesting, very interesting," he said to Aubrey, who was waving his wings in front of his beak to get rid of the dreadful smell of Clifford's burp.

"It tasted of cabbage, and the nettles stung my tongue a little bit. But there was also a strong taste of egg.

And it was much fizzier than I expected – there were lots of bubbles, of all different shapes and sizes. Hughie Curlew gave me a glass of red lemonade when I bought the gobstoppers from him the day your sister visited. That lemonade was sweet and full of bubbles. But your fizz wasn't at all sweet and the bubbles were completely different. I've never seen square and triangular bubbles until now. How did you make the drink?"

"Well, it started off as stinging nettle juice. You make that from stinging nettle leaves, water and a little sugar. Although clearly not enough sugar for your sweet bill," explained Aubrey.

"But how did you get the bubbles into it?" asked Clifford.

"Oh … er … I, er, I used a pump. A pump. Yes, a bicycle pump." As he said this, Aubrey turned bright pink and started to look very nervous.

"Really? That's not what I had expected," replied Clifford, now a little wary. "Tell me, what did you do with the pump?"

"Er … I, um, I just pumped it," blurted Aubrey. "That's it – I just pumped it."

"But there must have been more to it than that. I think you've been very clever, Aubs, getting the bubbles into the drink, and all I want to know is how you did it."

"Yes, well, it was like this…" began Aubrey, looking very unhappy. "I-I-I – oh dear!"

"Aubrey, you did use a bicycle pump, didn't you?" asked Walli.

"Yes, of course! Actually … no, I didn't. Oh dear. I'm terribly sorry. That was a little white lie." Aubrey looked as if he was about to burst into tears.

"Then how did you get the bubbles into the fizz?" asked Clifford, suddenly beginning to feel very concerned – and also rather sick.

Aubrey took a deep breath before he answered. "To be perfectly honest, Clifford, I'm not quite sure. When I made the stinging nettle juice, there wasn't enough room on the table to rest the saucepan, because my other drinks were already on it. Walli was using the remaining space to prepare the food. So I put it on the floor. I was wondering what to do next when I suddenly felt a big rumbling in my belly."

"OK, I'm with you so far," said Clifford. "Go on."

"For a moment I was very worried. I thought it would develop into a stomach ache, like the ones I've been having lately. But then I got lucky."

"Lucky? What do you mean?" asked Walli.

"Well, it wasn't the start of a stomach ache at all. It was just a great big farty-warty. It did smell very unpleasant, but luckily I was alone when I did it. You were in the garden digging for something. And Clifford was completely focused on preparing the games in the front room."

Clifford cleared his throat and looked straight at Aubrey. "And were you standing near the saucepan of stinging nettle juice when you did your farty-warty?"

"Yes, actually I was standing directly over it. Then I did some tidying up, and the odd thing was that when I next looked at the stinging nettle juice it had started to bubble and pop. I think my farty-warty must have somehow got mixed in with it. So I decided to call it stinging nettle fizz instead."

"Do you mean I just drank your bottom burp?" exploded Clifford. "That's why the stinging nettle fizz tasted of eggs! That's disgusting! I feel quite ill. It certainly wasn't good for my beak. Oooh, I need to think about something else, quickly, otherwise I'll have nightmares for weeks to come!"

Clifford stood quietly for a few seconds, composing himself. Walli and Aubrey looked at him with concern. After a couple of deep breaths and a few nervous, dry swallows, he was able to carry on. "What food did you make, Walli?" he asked.

"I thought I would make our favourites," said the warthog. "As you know, I love pepperoni pizza. So I decided to make that. Unfortunately Aubrey didn't have any flour to make the pizza base. So I cut out a circle from a cardboard box and used that as the base. Then I mashed up some tomatoes with my trotters and spread them on the cardboard. I put some grated stale cheese on top of the tomatoes and sprinkled on a little salt and pepper."

"And what about the pepperoni?" asked Clifford. "I know you love that."

"There wasn't any in the fridge. But I found something in the cupboard under the stairs earlier. It was a squashy oval of black stuff, so I went and got it and cut it into slices. It looks like small bits of pepperoni, although it tastes really nasty."

"How big was the bit of black stuff?" asked Aubrey, looking slightly embarrassed.

"About the size of a grape," replied Walli. "It looked pretty horrible and it had some small hairs stuck in it."

"Do you know what it was, Aubs?" asked Clifford.

"Yes, ear wax. My ear wax," replied Aubrey. "I was having a few problems hearing three or four days ago and suddenly, as I was searching in the cupboard for my cowboy boots, my left ear started to itch and this blob of wax fell out. It rolled into a corner and I left it there. It didn't look very nice. But the main thing is, I can hear clearly again."

"Hmm," said Clifford. "Walli, if you don't mind, I won't have any pizza. What food did you make for me?"

"I wanted to make you a big bowl of jelly snakes," answered Walli. "But Aubrey didn't have any jelly so I couldn't make them. So I decided to get some of your second-favourite things – witchetty grubs. I went into the garden and searched for them under the bush by the yew tree, where you showed me. But there weren't any there. Maybe they'd gone shopping or something. So I dug up some earthworms instead. They're almost the same as witchetty grubs, aren't they? There they are, wriggling in that bowl. Perhaps I should have washed the mud off them first."

"Great job, mate, really good tucker," said Clifford, smiling broadly at her. "And remember, Walli, it's the thought that counts."

"What did you make for me, Walli?" asked Aubrey hopefully.

"I know that you like sweetcorn and seeds and nuts and berries," said Walli. "But I didn't have enough time to look for those. So I picked you some grass. Is that OK? I'm only small and there's not much of me."

"Erm, yes, I suppose that will be fine," replied the disappointed turkey.

"Aubrey, do you think the party guests will like the food and drink we've made?" asked Walli nervously.

"Well, we've put a lot of effort in and there's lots of variety. So I hope so, Walli, I hope so."

"OK, guys, now the best bit," announced Clifford. "Come with me into the front room and I'll tell you all about the fantastic party games we'll be playing."

"Ooh, how exciting," squealed Walli, doing a little dance.

"Brilliant," said Aubrey as they followed Clifford. "What are they?"

"The first is pass the parcel, but with a difference. It's called pass the warthog. We wrap Walli up in lots of sheets of wrapping paper. If you don't have wrapping paper, then we can use newspaper. Everyone gathers in a circle. Then we play some music and pass her around. When the music stops – I'll be in control of that – the creature holding the parcel takes off a sheet of paper. Then the music starts again. This process continues until finally the lucky winner unwraps Walli."

"I don't like that idea," said Walli, her snout twitching with displeasure. "I don't want to be wrapped up in paper. I won't be able to see anything, and how will I be able to breathe?"

"Those are small and not hugely important details," said Clifford offhandedly, cross that his really good plan had been so quickly torpedoed. He hadn't expected Walli to object to his idea.

"Not to me they're not," said the warthog indignantly. "And what happens when a creature tears off the last sheet of paper and unwraps me?"

"They're allowed to keep you, of course," said Clifford, making it up as he went along. He hadn't really thought this game through properly. "They can take you home and you can be their pet. Or servant."

"I will not play this game!" said Walli crossly, stamping her trotters. And then she sat on the floor, looking very stubborn.

"OK, here's another idea," said Clifford. "This is a bit like pin the tail on the donkey, except it's called pin the tail on the warthog. It's a game of great skill. Creatures need to wear a blindfold to play."

Walli gave a snort of annoyance.

"And what would the tail be made of?" asked Aubrey.

"I'm not sure – probably a bit of rope with a big pin sticking through it," replied Clifford.

"I don't want a pin stuck in my bottom!" said Walli. "That's even worse than being wrapped up in paper!"

"Clifford, what happens if a creature manages to pin the tail on Walli's bottom?" asked Aubrey.

"The lucky creature is allowed to keep Walli and take her home. And then she becomes their pet, or servant," replied Clifford. "So it's a little bit like what happens in pass the parcel."

"It's exactly the same!" shrieked Walli. "I'm not going to play the pin-the-tail-on-the-warthog game either." And she wiggled her bottom on the floor and sat there with even greater determination.

"Boy, this is much harder than I thought," said Clifford quietly to himself. He turned to Walli. "Oh come on, mate, help us have some fun. OK, here is my best idea. Piñata!"

"Piñata?" said Aubrey. "I haven't heard of that before. What is it?"

"Well, normally you get some paper. You tear it into pieces and mix it with flour and water. This is called papier mâché. When it's still wet, you make it into the shape of a monster, like a dragon. You let it dry, then you paint it. Then you cut out a section from the top and fill the hollow shell full of sweets. You replace the section then hang the piñata from the ceiling with string. Then everyone hits it with sticks until it breaks open and all the sweets fall out. Everybody gets some and it's great fun."

"That sounds marvellous," said Aubrey. "So where is the papier mâché dragon?"

"Oh, I haven't made one. Remember, we don't have any flour for the papier mâché. What I thought we could do instead is to put some string around Walli and hang her from the ceiling. She looks a little bit like a monster. And as for the sweets – well, we could put one in her mouth. With the wrapper on, of course. Then after she has been hit with sticks, say ten times, she drops the sweet to the winning creature and the game ends. What do you think? A great idea, eh?"

"That's not a great idea at all," oinked a very worried Walli. "I don't want to be hit with sticks. And I don't look like a monster. Take it back, Clifford, and say you're sorry."

Clifford looked at Walli's sad little black eyes and immediately realised how horrid he had been to his friend. Walli trusted him and, with his careless behaviour, Clifford had betrayed her. He was filled with remorse. "I'm sorry, mate," he said, putting his right flipper on Walli's shoulder. "I wasn't thinking straight. It must be because I had a premonition about the stinging nettle fizz." Almost immediately another

enormous burp bubbled up inside Clifford and he couldn't help letting it out – straight into Walli's face. The little warthog turned green and almost fainted with the terrible smell.

After opening and closing his bill a few times to try to get rid of the unpleasant taste of the burp, Clifford turned to Aubrey. "What time do you make it?"

Aubrey looked at the grandfather clock. "It's 1.45pm. Crikey, everyone will be arriving soon. I'm so excited!"

"Me too!" said Clifford and Walli at the same time, the warthog having taken gulps of fresh air to clear her lungs. She looked at Clifford, he pulled a silly, friendly face, then they both laughed.

"This will be the best party ever," said Aubrey. "I wonder who will arrive first? Maybe Martha the Manatee. Or perhaps Georgina. I know, I bet it will be the Cloaked Croak – he's always at the front of the queue when there's free food and drink available."

Scene Three – The Waiting Game

The friends waited patiently for the first guest to arrive, Aubrey in the armchair and Clifford and Walli sitting on the floor next to him. The grandfather clock ticked loudly as they sat in silence. From time to time Aubrey got up and looked out of the window. But every time he came back shaking his head, muttering, "No one there."

Eventually, after what felt like forever, the clock struck 4pm. And still no one had arrived. Clifford looked at Aubrey. "Who did you say was coming to your party, mate?"

"It's a surprise party," replied Aubrey.

"Yes, I know that, but it was supposed to start two hours ago and still no one has arrived. So who are you expecting to come?"

"I don't know. It's a surprise party."

"Hang on, mate – did you actually invite any creatures?" asked Clifford. "Did you tell anyone that you were having a party?"

"No! As I keep saying, it's a surprise party."

"Oh Aubrey, oh dear. I think you've got a little bit confused," said Walli, shaking her head sadly. "Have you ever held a surprise party before?"

"No, this is my first time. I'm really looking forward to it and I can't wait to see who arrives."

"But Aubs, no one will arrive," said Clifford. "You need to tell your friends that you're having a party. That's how they know to turn up. Surprise parties are when lots of creatures arrange a party for one creature who doesn't know the party is going to happen. But you've done it the other way around, so it's not going to work."

The friends looked around the front room. The food and drink and games would all go to waste. There would be no party.

Clifford turned to Walli. "It's about time we were off, isn't it?" he said.

"Yes, you're quite right. We don't want to be late," replied Walli.

"What's happening? Where are you two going?" asked a puzzled Aubrey.

"To Douglas Duck's barbecue," said Clifford. "It starts at 4.30pm. He invited Walli and me when we met him in town the other day."

"Yes, it's going to be great fun," squealed Walli. "Martha will be bringing her delicious fruit salad and Hughie Curlew will be bringing lots of bottles of red lemonade."

"And everyone will be there," continued Clifford. "Georgina, Rina the Snow Monkey, Boris the Baboon, Purvis Pig, Geraldine the Jellyfish, Dr Dangle and lots of others. Even Washington Bear is coming up from Brusdor."

"Rick Rat is also coming," said Walli. "Although I know he's your deadliest enemy.

"Aubs – didn't Douglas invite you?" asked Clifford.

"No. He must have forgotten," replied Aubrey quietly. "And I thought he was my second-best friend…"

"Well, why don't you come with us anyway? Douglas won't mind. Come on, mate."

Aubrey put on a brave face, although inside he was deeply hurt that Douglas had not invited him. "No, it's OK. You two go and have fun. Don't worry about me. I'll just stay here on my own."

"Are you sure, Aubs?" asked Clifford. "The barbecue will be really cool."

"Yes, I'm certain," replied the gloomy turkey.

Clifford and Walli looked at each other, looked at Aubrey, then thought for a few seconds. Should they go or not? But it was no contest. They ran out through the front door and off down Fluffy Cloud Lane, laughing and shouting as they went.

Meanwhile Aubrey stood in his front room, looking around. His surprise party had been a disaster. Well, he might as well start clearing up. But then a tiny thought came into his head. As he stood there, the thought began to grow and grow until it was a great big solid-gold idea. A wicked smile appeared on his wizened old face.

He ran into the kitchen. In the cupboard under the sink, he found an empty bottle. He picked up the saucepan of stinging nettle fizz and carefully poured

the fizz into the bottle, making sure he didn't spill it – or smell it. Then he screwed on the cap tightly.

"Rick Rat will be there, will he?" muttered Aubrey quietly. "I bet he'll be thirsty. And I bet he'd love to have a drink of my special fizz!" With a sinister chuckle, Aubrey ran out of the front door, clutching the bottle. He could see Clifford and Walli in the distance. Shouting at the top of his voice, Aubrey headed after them. "Wait for me, guys, wait for me…"

TWO

NIL BY MOUTH

Island of Animaux location:

> » latitude 31° north
> » longitude 123° east

<small>Scene One – A Night to Remember</small>

The hour before dawn is the longest one of all. Or so it felt to Aubrey the Turkey as he tossed and turned in bed in his little house at the end of Fluffy Cloud Lane.

Aubrey had had a terrible night. He had gone to bed completely worn out after the excitement of his failed surprise party and then Douglas Duck's brilliant barbecue.

The barbecue had been particularly satisfying for Aubrey. He had arrived, desperately hoping that the awful Rick Rat would be fooled into taking a sip of his dubious stinging nettle fizz. But things had gone far better than Aubrey could ever have imagined. Rick had snatched the bottle from him, misguidedly thinking that he would annoy the turkey by doing so, and had guzzled the contents. Then Rick had laughed long and hard at Aubrey, believing that he had gained the upper paw. But then the greedy rat had swollen to five times his size as the secret gas that Aubrey had 'inserted' into the drink bubbled up inside him. This was swiftly followed by the first of many enormous, foul-smelling belches that Rick was quite helpless to prevent. The other creatures at the barbecue first observed, then smelt, Rick's eruptions, and quickly relegated him to the role of 'rattus non grata'. Everyone kept their distance from him. Rick slunk away in disgrace well before the evening was over, his legs only just able to support his ballooned body. But the worst was still to come for the rat. As he wallowed home, the gas suddenly caused him to

float high into the air, like a sausage-shaped airship. Unable to control his movements, Rick was swept west by a strong breeze, towards the coast and the endless sea beyond.

Aubrey had fallen into a deep sleep as soon as his head hit the pillow. But soon he awoke with a start. Something was wrong – very badly wrong. He lay there, wondering what it could be. There was nothing wrong with his house, as far as he could tell – downstairs seemed quiet and everything in his room seemed to be in order. His bedroom door was open as usual, and he could hear Clifford and Walli snoring in their bedroom. So nothing was wrong there either. He could see through his bedroom window, as he had forgotten to close the curtains, and it was a still, cloudless night with a beautiful crescent moon. Again, nothing wrong.

Aubrey had completed his checklist and all was well. But then he realised there was one check he hadn't carried out. And that was the very important check on himself. As soon as he remembered this, Aubrey quickly became aware why he had woken up. It was because of the terrible pain in his tummy. It was the worst pain he had ever experienced – much worse than when he had had a bad belly before. There was an overall dull pain that made him feel quite sick, coupled with a sharp stabbing pain that pulsed horribly on his right-hand side. It was so bad that he was actually gasping for breath.

"If I lie quietly and pretend I'm not in pain, then it will get bored and go away," he rationalised, without any basis.

But after lying still for many hours, Aubrey finally realised it was no good. The pain, both the dull and the sharp forms, persisted, and even seemed to be getting worse. Knowing that he couldn't ignore things any longer, Aubrey called out to his friends. "Walli, Clifford. Could you come and see me? I don't feel very well and I'm scared."

Being a light sleeper, in case a lion ever tried to sneak up on her, Walli heard Aubrey. She quickly got up and trotted into his bedroom. Clifford, being a heavy sleeper, continued to snooze as he chased jelly snakes in the Land of Nod.

"Howzit, Aubrey. What's the matter?" asked the warthog, concerned because Aubrey usually slept soundly and had never called out in the night before.

"It's my tummy. I've got a terrible pain. It really hurts!" gasped the turkey, in absolute agony and finding it difficult to speak clearly.

"How long have you had it?" replied Walli, turning on the light then jumping onto the bed and looking at Aubrey.

"I don't know. I woke up with it. It's much worse than the pains I have had in the past. I don't know what to do. Can you help me, Walli, please?"

Walli gave her friend a gentle smile, although secretly she was very worried, as Aubrey's face was ashen and he was sweating profusely. He looked really ill.

"Of course I will help you. Shall I call Dr Dangle?"

"I don't think that's the best idea," said Clifford, walking into the room. He had been woken up by Aubrey's bedroom light, which shone down the corridor and into the back bedroom. Like Walli, Clifford saw that Aubrey was looking very ill. He had never seen him like this before and he knew that something was badly wrong with his friend. He was as worried as Walli.

"It will take Dr Dangle too long to arrive. Aubs, I think we should phone for an ambulance. What's the number of the emergency services?"

"It's 999. But do you really think we need to call them? Isn't that a bit dramatic? And they might be cross."

Clifford looked at the turkey. "They won't be cross. It's better to be safe than sorry, mate. The ambulance crew will be able to assess you, to see why you're feeling ill. If they think you're OK, then no harm done. But if they think you need to go to hospital, then they can take you there straight away."

"OK, Clifford," replied Aubrey. "But could

you phone them as soon as possible? The pain has suddenly got even worse!"

Clifford rushed out of the room and down the stairs into the sitting-room, where he dialled 999. After taking the address and some details about Aubrey's condition, the operator told Clifford that the ambulance would arrive in less than ten minutes.

Walli and Clifford sat with Aubrey, keeping him company, until the ambulance arrived. They heard its siren first then noticed the blue flashing lights as it stopped outside the house.

Clifford went down the stairs again to let the ambulance crew in. There were two crew members, both with beautiful green plumage – they were obviously parrot-medics. After taking some brief details from the platypus they rushed up the stairs, wearing backpacks full of medical equipment and carrying a stretcher between them.

"Now then, Aubrey," said Pranoy the Parrot, "where do you hurt?"

"It's my belly," gasped Aubrey. "The pain is continuing to get worse. Please do something."

"Now then, Aubrey," said Patrick the Parrot, "where do you hurt?"

"Hang on, mate. Didn't your colleague just ask the same question?" said a surprised Clifford.

"Just double-checking," replied Patrick the Parrot.

"Just double-checking," replied Pranoy the Parrot.

After what seemed an eternity of twice-asked questions, plus double examinations, the parrots agreed that Aubrey was indeed very ill. They carefully helped him onto the stretcher and then, rather less carefully, carried him down the stairs, almost dropping him twice. Outside, they loaded him into the back of the ambulance, allowed Walli to come with him to keep him company, then slammed the doors and headed off at high speed to Wincot General Hospital, the blues and twos flashing and wailing.

Clifford locked up the house, climbed aboard Aubrey's skateboard and headed after the ambulance at a speed that even he thought was much too fast.

Scene Two – The Turkey's Darkest Hour

At the hospital, the casualty department was having a very busy night. Creatures who had come in with minor problems, including small flesh wounds from excessive scratching, cracked toenails, and worm and lice infestations, were jostling for position, thinking that each of them was the sickest and deserved to be seen first.

The parrot-medics brought Aubrey in from the ambulance on a trolley, and he patiently waited his turn. With Pranoy the Parrot's help, Walli climbed onto the trolley to hold the turkey's wing and keep him company. Shortly afterwards Clifford came over too, having left the skateboard and its smoking, glowing, red-hot wheels outside the casualty department main door. He too climbed on the trolley.

The three were then joined by another creature, who had wandered over from the main waiting area.

But this was one creature that none of them was pleased to see.

"Well, if it isn't old Aubrey, with his two mangy buddies," said Rick Rat, scampering up the trolley leg and sitting at the far end of the trolley, facing them. For some reason, he was carrying a large rock. The rodent was clearly delighted to see the turkey in so much distress.

"Go away, Rick, we don't want to talk to you," said Walli, still cross with the rat about the yellow card he had given her in the cup final.

"I wasn't talking to you, wart-face," said Rick with his customary rudeness. He fixed his nasty, beady little eyes on Aubrey. "What's wrong, turkey? Feeling a little under the weather?" And then Rick laughed – a nasty, high-pitched squeaking kind of laugh.

"I've got a terrible pain in my tummy," said Aubrey, wishing with all his heart that both the pain and Rick would go away. "And get off my trolley. I didn't invite you to sit on it."

"It's not your trolley – it belongs to the hospital. I've got just as much right to sit on it as you do," countered the rat. "A pain in your tummy, eh? It serves you right. I wouldn't be surprised if you had to go under the knife before the night is over. The surgeon will be slitting you open and rummaging around in your guts. And they'll probably throw away most of what they find because it sounds like you've gone rotten inside!"

Studying the look of terror on Aubrey's face that his words had caused, Rick continued. "Wow, look at your eyes, Aubrey! They have started to bulge – perhaps in fear? Or maybe that's just another symptom of your rottenness. I imagine the surgeon will need to take them out as well. He'll probably scoop them out with a spoon."

"And why are you here, Rick?" interrupted Clifford, fed up with the rat's offensive behaviour. "You're still swollen to twice your normal size. Remind me, didn't you swell up after you had been greedy and drunk all of Aubrey's stinging nettle fizz?"

Rick glared at him. "If you must know, fish-face, I nearly died after drinking the fizz. It made me float away, right over to Singsong Bay. I would have been blown out to sea if Claude Crane Fly hadn't stopped flying around the lighthouse to rescue me. He carried me to the shore and gave me this rock to hold. It's the only thing that's keeping me on the ground. I dare not let go of it!"

Clifford had noticed the rock and had assumed the rat had adopted it as a pet, since so few other creatures wanted to be his friend.

Rick continued his tale of woe. "The actual reason I'm here is because I'm suffering from an ingrowing tail. It happened after you kicked the ball at me when I was refereeing the cup final. So it's all your fault. Also, ever since I drank the fizz I can't stop burping – and they have the most revolting eggy taste and smell."

"Well, Rick, you have nothing to worry about," said Clifford, deciding it was time to take the wind out of the rat's sails. "Your treatment will be very simple. The surgeon will first cut off your tail with a carving knife and will then stick a knitting needle in you, to let all the gas out. By the way, do you know where the gas came from? It's from the fizz. And do you know what made the fizz fizz? Aubrey farted into it. And so you're full of Aubrey's fart, and that's what you can taste. I must say, it couldn't have happened to a nicer rat!"

Having delivered his punchline, Clifford burst out laughing. Walli joined in and even Aubrey, despite his pain, was able to titter a little. Rick slunk away, down from the trolley and back to the general waiting area, humiliated but more determined than ever to pay Aubrey back one day.

The friends continued to wait patiently. Creatures carried on arriving and departing, most still with minor injuries but some with serious conditions. There was high drama when Zoe Zebra was wheeled in. She was taken straight to the delivery room where she gave birth to a gorgeous healthy foal who, after careful thought, she named Zac.

Although he was still in great pain, Aubrey's greediness began to get the better of him. "I'm ever so slightly peckish, and I think it's breakfast time. I wonder if either of you could see if there's a shop in the hospital that sells tasty treats for a poor, sick turkey? Perhaps one that sells cream cakes, cheese-and-onion pasties, sweets and red lemonade?"

"Aubs, I'm surprised at you," said Clifford. "Food is the last thing you should be thinking about at the moment. Besides, can't you see that sign on the wall over there? It says all creatures waiting to be examined should be 'nil by mouth'. That means no eating."

"But I haven't got a mouth. I've got a beak," replied Aubrey, hoping that this would somehow exempt him from the rule.

Clifford smiled at him. "It's the same thing, mate. It's the same thing."

At last Aubrey was seen. Nurse Narwal, who was standing in a full water butt to keep her moist, assessed him then Surgeon Scorpion, the finest sawbones on the whole of Animaux, confirmed her diagnosis. "You're suffering from acute appendicitis, Aubrey," he explained. "From what you told me as I examined you, it sounds like your appendix has been grumbling for quite a while."

"So what's the treatment?" asked Aubrey, trying to look brave but secretly absolutely terrified. "Will I need to take five witchetty grubs, or perhaps even ten?"

"Witchetty grubs are no use for appendicitis," replied the scorpion, blowing some strands of cotton wool off one of his pincers. "I need to operate without delay. If your appendix bursts, you could die."

"Die? Really? Do you mean it?" gasped Aubrey, almost unable to believe what he had been told.

"Yes, it's that serious. We need to get going. Nurse Narwal will prepare you – she will shave the feathers off your tummy and will bring you to the operating theatre. I will then operate. But don't worry – it should be a simple procedure and I should be finished in less than an hour. You can watch me, if you like. I'll ask the nurse to hold up a mirror so you can see me as I cut you open, fight through the layers of fat and rivers of blood, then remove your appendix."

"Surgeon Scorpion, can I ask you a question?" said Clifford, suddenly a little concerned after hearing what the scorpion had said.

"Of course," replied the scorpion. "What would you like to know?"

"Won't you be giving Aubrey a general anaesthetic for the operation, so he will sleep through it?"

Surgeon Scorpion gave a little smile. Clifford's question was a good one. "No, that is not necessary. I will just give him a light sting on the tummy with my tail. That should make him numb. And it's much less dangerous than a general anaesthetic. In rare cases creatures can have a bad reaction to the sting. For example, Selwyn the Shark changed from being a sweet, oversized fish to the most dangerous criminal on Animaux. But Aubrey should be all right."

Clifford wasn't sure he agreed, but he decided to bow to the medic's superior knowledge. And at the same time he made a mental note to take good care of himself, to avoid ever needing to become a patient of Surgeon Scorpion.

A teary-eyed Aubrey turned to his friends as Nurse Narwal splashed about in the water butt next to him, ready to prepare him for his operation.

"I'm so frightened. What if everything doesn't go well? What if Surgeon Scorpion finds other things wrong with me, apart from my bad appendix? Maybe I am all rotten inside, like Rick said."

"Aubs, you're in the best place, mate. This seems like a really nice hospital and the medical team seem first-rate." Clifford gave Nurse Narwal a friendly smile as he said this, and she returned the compliment. "And forget about Rick," he continued. "He was talking his usual rubbish."

"Don't worry, Aubrey," said Walli. "We'll be staying and we'll see you after your operation is over. And we'll look after you really well over the next few weeks, until you're completely recovered."

"Thank you both," replied the turkey, feeling much more at ease. "I am so lucky to have you as my friends." He looked at Nurse Narwal. "Nurse, can we begin, please? I'd like to get this over with as soon as possible."

Walli and Clifford jumped down from the trolley just as the turtle orderlies (Tim, Tom, Ted and Tina) positioned themselves under Nurse Narwal's water butt. They were able to inch the butt forward despite the enormous weight they were carrying, allowing Nurse Narwal to push Aubrey's trolley into the preparation room.

"He will be OK, won't he?" Walli asked Clifford.

"He's as tough as old boots," replied Clifford. "He'll be fine. I think we're the ones in trouble – I can see him being a difficult patient as he recovers at home, and I'm sure we'll be rushing around, seeing to his every need!"

The friends smiled at each other and sat patiently in the waiting area as Surgeon Scorpion sharpened his scalpel.

Fortunately, the operation went without a hitch. Aubrey chose *not* to watch everything in a mirror.

After two days on a ward, he was well enough to

go home. Aubrey had asked for his appendix to be put in a jar so he could take it home with him and get other creatures to pay him a silver dollar to look at it. But Walli had objected to the idea of the appendix being in the house, so Aubrey abandoned the idea.

As Clifford had predicted, Aubrey was very demanding when he got home. He lay in bed and insisted that he was given a bell, so he could ring it every time he needed something. And ring it he did – at all hours of the day and night. He rang it for food, he rang it to be brought something to read, he rang it to ask for his pillows to be plumped up – he even rang it to ask Walli and Clifford what they were doing. But the worst ring, the special, persistent *ding-ding, ding-ding, ding-ding* one, was when he wanted the dressing on his stitches changed. This disagreeable task always fell to poor Walli; Clifford was always mysteriously 'unavailable' whenever the bell sounded.

Aubrey received many visitors while he recovered. Georgina the Goat and Douglas Duck put in regular appearances, as did Martha the Manatee, who always brought a basket of delicious food with her. Aubrey made sure that he ate most of the contents, leaving only a few pie crusts, apple cores and banana skins for Walli and Clifford.

Aubrey's sister Audrey came up for the day from Brusdor. She was nice to all of them and even joked with Clifford about the witchetty grubs he had put in her bags. However, all Aubrey, Walli and Clifford remembered about her visit was that she had sprayed on too much nasty-smelling perfume. The fragrance got into their eyes and mouths and affected their sense of taste for a long time.

Dr Dangle attended two weeks after Aubrey had arrived home. Happy with how the wound on Aubrey's tummy had healed, he snipped off the stitches and told the turkey he could now get up and take care of himself. But Aubrey, being a truly lazy bird, had enjoyed being waited on by Clifford and Walli and he managed to get them to take care of him for another week by not telling them what Dr Dangle had said. Clifford only found out about Aubrey's deception after bumping into Dr Dangle on Wincot High Street. To show their annoyance at having been used by Aubrey, neither Walli nor Clifford spoke to him for many days afterwards.

Scene Three – *Radix Malorum…*

One evening a week later Walli and Clifford were sitting at the kitchen table, having just enjoyed a tasty tea of beans on toast.

"I suppose Aubs will be down in a minute and will expect us to cook something for him to eat."

"It's OK. I don't mind preparing something for him," replied Walli. "Although he was very naughty, pretending to be ill for longer than he was, let's not forget that he was very sick when he went to the hospital. I think we're lucky to still have him with us."

Clifford nodded, but he wasn't finished. "Don't you think he has changed since his operation – and not for the best? The way he talks to us and treats us, the fact that he keeps muttering to himself and then laughing?"

"I had noticed," said Walli. "But I had hoped that he would start to return to normal."

Clifford held up a flipper. "Shh. He's coming down the stairs. Let's talk about it later."

Aubrey walked into the kitchen and sat at the table, opposite them. "Walli and Clifford," he began. "My recent grave illness has put things into sharper perspective. None of us knows how much time we have left."

"What are you talking about?" said Clifford, thinking that Aubrey was starting to get maudlin and wanting to avoid being sucked under his dark cloud.

Aubrey continued. "I have been giving this a lot of thought. In fact, I have been thinking more deeply than either of you could ever understand. My conclusion, having come so close to death, is that life is for living. And life is for winners. Let the losers be satisfied with the breadcrumbs! This turkey is going places. I will soon be enjoying the finest things that life has to offer."

"You're rambling, Aubs," replied Clifford, wondering what on earth his feathered friend was talking about. "Perhaps this is an after-effect of your recent surgery, but you're not making any sense."

"Let me try to be clearer, dear platypus. When I was young I always thought that at this point in my life I would be wealthy. That I would have more gold and silver coins than I could ever possibly spend, and that all the creatures of Animaux would admire me for my intelligence, good looks and enormous charm." Aubrey paused briefly, then he steamed ahead. "And yet here I am, with only two silver dollars to my name and with two lodgers who don't pay me any rent! But it is not too late to change things. I have spotted a gap in the market and I intend to take full advantage of it."

Walli looked at Clifford. The platypus shrugged, crossed his eyes and stuck out his tongue, clearly indicating that he thought Aubrey had gone mad.

Aubrey noticed him and took offence. "Mad, am I? I'll show you who's mad! Do you remember when I gave Godfrey the Giant Tortoise a button from my cardigan and said it was a gold eagle? He believed me, and it was only out of the goodness of my own heart that I replaced it with a real one."

Walli and Clifford gasped, remembering what had *really* happened.

"Clearly I have a talent for tricking other creatures, for passing off something that is not valuable as something that is. There are lots of creatures on Animaux with bad eyesight or who are a bit silly – they can also be tricked. So my great plan is to forge money and then spend it as though it is real! I will cut out round shapes from the metal baking trays in the bottom of the oven then paint them with gold and silver paint. You see before you a true criminal mastermind!" Aubrey gave a short triumphant gobble. The announcement of his plan had made him dizzy with excitement, and he was enjoying the sensation.

Clifford briefly reflected on what Aubrey had said, then gave his honest opinion. "Mate, the only gap you've found is one in your brain. You're back to your old tricks: thinking about doing dishonest things, including cheating some of the more vulnerable creatures on Animaux. Walli and I have warned you about this before, but you seem to have forgotten. Let me share something with you. When I was in Oz I read a book written by a human called Chaucer. It included stories about some travellers, and one of the tales was about a human who loved money more than anything else. Sounds a bit like you, doesn't it? The human fooled other humans into giving him money. The moral was '*radix malorum est cupiditas*,' or, in more modern words, that the love of money is the root of all evil."

"You're talking nonsense, ducky-wucky," Aubrey snapped rudely. "The love of money is good and my plan will see me rich beyond my wildest dreams. But I won't be sharing any of it with piglet or you."

"Aubrey!" squealed Walli, very cross with him.

"How dare you speak to Clifford and me like this? We're your friends and we've just looked after you when you were ill. You are the most ungrateful turkey and you should feel ashamed of yourself. Say you're sorry!"

"And let me make you a promise, Aubs," continued Clifford. "It is illegal and immoral to forge money and then try to spend it. If you do this, then I will tell the Crow Police. And they are not creatures to get on the wrong side of! Also, in case you've forgotten, remember that Selwyn the Shark was convicted of forging money and he is still languishing in DeepDarkHole Prison."

Without giving Aubrey a chance to reply, Clifford and Walli decided it was time to go to bed. They left the table in silence and went up the stairs. When they reached the top of the stairs, Walli stopped and spoke to her friend. "What do you think has happened to Aubrey to explain why he has been so horrible since leaving hospital?"

"I think he's having a bad reaction to Surgeon Scorpion's sting and this has caused his behaviour to change. He needs to have an antidote so that he returns to normal – whatever Aubs' 'normal' is,"

replied Clifford. He had clearly thought the matter through. "I'll speak to Dr Dangle tomorrow, see if he's got any ideas about it."

And then the friends trotted and hopped down the corridor to their beds.

Meanwhile, downstairs in the kitchen Aubrey smouldered and chuntered to himself. Just as Clifford thought, the turkey was fully in the grip of a madness caused by an adverse reaction to Surgeon

Scorpion's sting. The old gobbler had become paranoid.

His focus was on Walli and Clifford. The two creatures he had thought were his friends had called him ungrateful and had threatened to report him to the Crow Police. He would not be able to forget or forgive these insults quickly. And tomorrow would present the perfect opportunity for him to wreak revenge.

THREE

OPEN WIDE

Island of Animaux location:

» latitude 21° north

» longitude 82° west

SCENE ONE – AUBREY'S CURTAIN CALL

"So how much are they worth?" asked Aubrey as he stood in Douglas Duck's curtain shop, impatiently tapping the tip of his left wing on the counter. "Come on, Douglas, hurry up and give me a price. I haven't got all day."

Ignoring Aubrey's bad manners, Douglas once again looked at the curtains that the turkey had brought in to sell. Normally he would never buy second-hand curtains, but Aubrey was a friend and Douglas might be prepared to make an exception. But only if Aubrey had a good reason for wanting to sell the curtains.

"They're rather tatty," said Douglas. "Look, there are holes here, and here. And the colour has faded. The sunlight has caused that to happen. I don't

remember seeing these in your house before. Which windows were they on?"

"They're from the back bedroom, the one that Clifford and Walli share," said Aubrey. "The curtains in the rest of the house are nicer, but I need all of those. Especially the ones in my bedroom, because without those I would have no privacy."

"But what about Clifford's and Walli's privacy?" asked Douglas, frowning. "Without curtains you'll be able to see into their bedroom at night when the light is on and they will be woken early each morning by the rising sun. What did they say when you told them you were selling their curtains?"

"Look, Douglas, they're my curtains, from my house," said Aubrey sourly. "I haven't told them. They were playing in the garden – my garden – as usual when I took the curtains down, and I decided not to say anything to them. I thought I'd leave it as a surprise. They've probably found out by now." Aubrey chuckled quietly to himself. He was still firmly in the grip of the madness caused by his bad reaction to Surgeon Scorpion's sting. "But who cares?" he continued. "Now, back to my earlier question. How much are the curtains worth?"

Douglas looked at Aubrey with a feeling of despair. His friend could be so callous and unfeeling. And he was worse than ever at the moment. Douglas wanted to tell his friend this, but when he was feeling a little braver. So not today.

"Before I give you a price, Aubrey, can I ask why you need the money so badly? Is everything OK in your little house at the end of Fluffy Cloud Lane?"

Aubrey hadn't expected Douglas to ask this question, and for a moment he didn't know what to say. But, being a sneaky and cheating old bird, he soon came up with a completely untruthful, yet believable answer.

"It's so I can buy some food for Walli's and Clifford's tea. I don't want them to go to bed with empty tummies," he said, trying as hard as possible to look honest. But although he was used to giving dishonest answers and generally swindling other creatures – indeed, he was quite an expert in this area – for some reason this time Aubrey felt slightly guilty and so he didn't look Douglas in the eye as he spoke.

"Oh, is that the reason?" said Douglas with relief. "Then of course I will buy the curtains from you. I wouldn't want Walli and Clifford to go hungry. Look, here are four silver dollars. That's much more than the curtains are worth, but it should be enough for you to get some good food and give them a very nice meal. You are a good turkey, Aubrey, and I am proud to be your friend."

"Thanks, Douglas. You are very kind," said Aubrey, sweeping the coins off the counter and into his wing.

"And how is your tummy at the moment, Aubrey? Are you quite recovered after your recent operation?"

"I'm right as rain, Douglas – in fact, I've never felt better. But I can't spend all day chatting with you. I've got Walli and Clifford to take care of. I'm going straight to Maureen Moose's Mini Mart to buy some delicious food for the two of them – such sweet creatures – and also a little – although much less – for me. So I'll be off."

"Enjoy, Aubrey. Enjoy," said a smiling Douglas, pleased that he had done his good deed for the day. He would sleep easy that night. And then he began to wonder whether he should set up a charity. A charity that would provide help for the needy creatures of Animaux. The Douglas Duck Charity. But then he quickly changed his mind when he realised that Aubrey would always be first in the queue when benefits were given out.

Aubrey left Douglas's shop, the hint of a spring in his step. But instead of turning right towards Maureen's shop he turned left. As he strutted down the street, a thoroughly malevolent look on his lined old face, Aubrey couldn't resist congratulating himself about his latest deception. "Douglas is a silly old sucker," he cackled disgracefully. "I'll not spend his silver dollars on Clifford and Walli. No tea for them tonight! No, this money will be spent on my best friend. And my best friend is me!"

Getting quite carried away with his self-perceived cleverness, Aubrey continued to chunter. "I have triumphed again! Once more I have proved how smart I am and how inferior all the other creatures are compared to me. I deserve to be President, no – make that King! Now there's a thought…"

Flushed with his misguided sense of self-importance, Aubrey rushed on, completely ignoring Rina the Snow Monkey who was coming from the opposite direction and who had stopped to say a friendly hello to him.

He was heading for Hughie Curlew's sweet shop. Not exactly the place to buy delicious food. Although the sweets were pretty good.

"Four silver dollars should be plenty." He chuckled as he went, lengthening his stride to reach the shop as quickly as possible. "I will soon be able to fulfil my lifelong ambition – or at least the one I have had since getting out of bed this morning."

And so what was the latest on the long and ever-growing scroll of Aubrey's 'bucket list' ambitions?

Well, it was very simple, really. He wanted to buy as many chocolate-covered sweets as possible, take them home and stuff them one after another into his beak until they were all gone. And then he would sit in his armchair with sweet wrappers all over the floor and chocolate all over his face. And this would make him happy. Although quite why Aubrey thought this would make him happy, only he could say.

In just a few more steps Aubrey had reached Hughie Curlew's. As he entered the shop, the doorbell made its usual jangling noise.

"Morning, Hughie," Aubrey gobbled to the curlew, who was putting a jar of sugar canes and some bottles of red lemonade back onto one of the many full shelves in the shop.

"Top of the morning. But who is it?" said Hughie, turning around to face Aubrey, peering uncertainly through his glasses, which had thick – and, on this occasion, very dirty – lenses. Hughie had been meaning to clean them for some time, but the lenses were so smudged that he couldn't see well enough to find a cloth or tissue.

"Ha, ha. A good customer," replied Aubrey, rubbing the silver dollars together as he spoke. "It's me, Aubrey. And today, Hughie, I want to put in a big order for some of your finest chocolate-covered fancies. The ones with the assorted centres that you make in your kitchen."

"You're in luck, Aubrey," said Hughie, with his usual mellifluous Irish burr. "For I made a new batch this morning and they're just grand. Hang on, I'll get them." He disappeared through a door at the back of the shop and a few seconds later re-emerged with a tray containing exactly fifty chocolate fancies, which had been carefully wrapped in red, green, blue and gold foil.

"There's all the usual flavours, including raspberry, coffee and orange creams, grapefruit twist, nut crunch, and a single toffee supreme," announced Hughie proudly.

Aubrey looked at the tray, his eyes bigger than saucers, and dribbled slightly. "Gorgeous, just gorgeous," he mumbled, hardly able to get the words out because of his excitement. "I'll take the lot."

"What, all of them?" said Hughie, surprised. "But what about the other creatures, such as Godfrey the Giant Tortoise? They always like to buy one or two of my chocolates to brighten their day. And I won't be making any more for at least a week."

"Let them go without. I need them all," said the greedy turkey. "Is something wrong with my money, Hughie? Not good enough for you or something?"

"Your money is fine," replied Hughie. "It's just

that I don't see it very often because you're usually so mean – sorry, careful – with it. Anyway, you asked for the chocolates first, so you can have them. I'll put them in a paper bag and then I need to weigh it, to work out the price. Wait a minute."

Aubrey watched intently as Hughie went about his work. Finally, the moment of truth arrived. "That's 1.2 kilos in total and that comes to three dollars and seventy five cents, please."

Aubrey flipped the four dollar coins onto the counter. One rolled off and landed on the floor behind it. Hughie heard it drop and bent down to try and find it.

"Don't worry about that now, Hughie," said Aubrey. "You can find it later. I'm in a hurry to get home and feast, so just give me my change and I'll be off."

Hughie did as he was asked. He gave Aubrey some copper cent coins then showed his appreciation for the turkey's purchase. "Thanks a million. Enjoy the chocolates."

Aubrey grunted a reply and left the shop, clutching the bag to his chest, pleased that he had enough change to afford a taxi ride home.

SCENE TWO – CHOCS AWAY

In the front room of the little house at the end of Fluffy Cloud Lane Walli and Clifford were comparing the length, thickness and general beauty of their tails when Aubrey burst through the door.

"G'day, Aubs," said Clifford, looking up. "Where have you been, and what's in the bag?"

"None of your business and none of your business," replied the turkey rudely, without looking at him.

"Strewth, you are a ray of sunshine today, aren't you, mate?" said Clifford, shaking his head in disapproval.

Aubrey ignored him. Instead he went over to his armchair and parked his big fat turkey bottom in the middle of the worn, stained cushion. He was still clutching the paper bag.

"Aubrey, I was in our bedroom earlier," said Walli. "And I noticed that our curtains have been taken down. What has happened to them?"

"I've sold them to Douglas Duck," said Aubrey, unwrapping a chocolate and popping it in his beak. "I tricked him earlier by saying I needed to sell them to get money for food for you two. He gave me far too much for them!"

"And what are we supposed to use in place of the curtains?" asked Clifford.

"Stick up some sheets of newspaper if you must, although you'll need to buy it."

"And did you buy us some food, like you told Douglas you would?" asked Walli hopefully, looking at the bag that Aubrey was holding. "There's no food in the kitchen and my little tummy is empty and has been rumbling all morning."

"No, of course I didn't buy any food," replied Aubrey curtly. "I used the money to buy some sweets. Correction, it was to buy *me* some sweets. Chocolate fancies, to be precise. I've cleared out Hughie Curlew's entire stock!"

"But what about us?" asked Clifford.

"Oh, there's nothing in this bag for you or old warty-face. This is all for me." With that, Aubrey unwrapped another chocolate and popped it in his beak. "Two down, forty-eight to go. What joy," he gobbled happily. Then Aubrey looked at the surprised, sad expressions on his friends' faces. He gave a small sigh and nodded slightly.

Perhaps he was having a change of heart. Perhaps he was about to show that he could be kind. Clifford and Walli waited expectantly.

"Oh, all right. You can have any chocolates that I don't like. Hang on a minute – this is a coconut one. I can't stand those." Aubrey fished the half-chewed chocolate out of his beak and tossed it in Clifford's and Walli's direction. It landed on the floor in front of them, immediately picking up dust and fluff. They looked at it with disgust.

"Help yourselves," said Aubrey with a cruel laugh.

"That's just horrible!" snorted Walli angrily.

"No, it should be fine," said Aubrey. "Just rinse it under the tap in the kitchen and it will be as good as new."

"You are the most selfish, greedy creature I've ever met," quackled an extremely cross Clifford. "Go ahead and eat all of your sweets, you mangy bird. I hope they make you sick."

Clifford looked at Walli. "Come on, mate. Let's go into the kitchen and look in the fridge and through all the cupboards to see if we've missed anything that we could eat. Perhaps we'll be lucky."

As they left the room, Aubrey settled back in

his armchair and proceeded to unwrap and eat every one of the remaining chocolates, some two or even three at a time. As each of the chocolates disappeared into his beak, down his throat and into his quickly swelling belly, he threw the wrappers on the floor.

"Walli and Clifford can clear those up later," he schemed. "I'll save one coffee cream for both of them to share as payment, because I don't really like them either." He chuckled out loud.

After a lot of unwrapping and an equal amount of gluttony, Aubrey came to the last chocolate. It was the only one with a gold wrapper, and he had put it to one side as it was his favourite. It was the toffee supreme. He was looking forward to rolling it around in his beak and savouring it before chewing it. Perhaps he would even go into the kitchen, to show Clifford and Walli how much he was enjoying it.

He popped it into his beak and licked it, enjoying the chocolate coating and the sugary caramel taste from the toffee beneath.

Then he bit into it.

Immediately, he screamed. The most terrible scream ever heard on the Island of Animaux.

Meanwhile, in the kitchen Walli and Clifford had managed to find a single dried pea on the floor behind the fridge. They were wondering how to cook it. But however they cooked it, they hoped it would taste nice. Although it wouldn't be very filling. And it would taste of pea, and they weren't very keen on peas. But it would do. It had to.

But all thoughts of the pea vanished from their minds when they heard Aubrey's scream. They rushed back into the front room.

"Whatever has happened?" squealed Walli, quite alarmed.

"Ib by doof," gurgled Aubrey, chocolate and toffee-coloured saliva oozing out of the sides of his beak as he spoke.

Walli and Clifford looked at each other, mystified.

"Say again? I didn't get that," said Clifford. "Are you speaking in Turkese?"

"I said 'ib by doof. In by beak'," mumbled Aubrey, desperately hoping they would understand.

"Oh – I think he's got a problem with one of his teeth," said Walli.

"I see!" said Clifford. "Come on then, mate, open your beak and let's take a look. Walli, while I'm fishing around inside Aubs' beak, can you go into the cupboard under the stairs and get the hammer and chisel from Aubs' toolbox? I may need them."

"No!" shouted Aubrey, alarmed. He breathed deeply and composed himself. This seemed to help him speak more clearly. "You're not looking in my beak, Clifford – it's private and not for your eyes or flippers." Aubrey turned to Walli. "I need to go to the dentist straight away. Will you come with me, to hold my wing while I get examined? Please?"

"Of course I will," said Walli. "But who is the dentist?"

"It's Sadie the Stick Insect. She's got a practice in Wincot, near the town hall."

Clifford looked at Aubrey and shook his head, tutting. "You know, all this is your own fault," he said. "I have no sympathy for you. You should be taking good care of yourself after your recent operation. But that seems furthest from your mind. I see you've scoffed all the chocolates and that will have done your tummy no good, or your weight. And it certainly will not have been good for your teeth. Talking of which, I've noticed that you don't have a toothbrush – at least, you don't keep one in the bathroom. So obviously you don't clean your teeth, and that's another reason your breath always smells nasty."

This was quite a tsunami of criticism for Aubrey to face. But as it washed over him, he fired straight back. "I'll eat what I want when I want to. And when did you become an expert on teeth? Tell me, smarty pants, how do you keep your teeth clean?"

"Platypuses don't have teeth. But I make sure I keep my bill in shape by flossing it every morning with the laces of your football boots."

"So that's why they're always soggy! Anyway, at least I've got teeth to go bad and give me toothache," said Aubrey, trying to occupy the high ground. "And in my book that means I'm better than you. One-nil to me, I think, quackpot."

Clifford counter-attacked. "You won't look so clever when the dentist is drilling away at your bad tooth. Perhaps they'll even need to pull it out! I'd say that was one-all, wouldn't you?"

Seeing that trouble was brewing, Walli rushed between Aubrey and Clifford as they glared at each other. "You two stop squabbling," she ordered. "Just calm down. Come on, let's go and visit Sadie. Hopefully she will be able to see you quickly, Aubrey."

SCENE THREE – IN THE DENTIST'S CHAIR

They arrived at Sadie's dental surgery after a forty-minute walk into town, Aubrey moaning and groaning about his bad tooth all the way.

In fact, Sadie had no problem seeing Aubrey as soon as they arrived. This was because all the creatures on Animaux ate sensibly and as a consequence had very good teeth. Therefore, Sadie didn't have many patients, except for normal check-ups, so anyone who did arrive as an emergency filled her with excitement.

"Ah, Aubrey," she said as the friends came in. "I haven't seen you since you were a chick. What's wrong?"

"I've got a bad tooth and it's really hurting," replied the pained turkey.

"Hmm," murmured Sadie. "Sit down in my examining chair and I'll take a look."

Aubrey did as he was told. As he sat down, Sadie pulled a lever to tilt the chair back to give her a better view of his mouth. "Open wide," she said, turning on a bright light to shine into the turkey's beak. "When did you last visit a dentist, Aubrey?"

"The last time I was here."

"Well, in future try to go at least every six months. That's good practice." Sadie briefly looked across the room. "Who are your friends, Aubrey? I don't think I've seen them before."

"Clifford Platypus and Walli Hogg," gurgled a horrified Aubrey as Sadie started to feel inside his mouth with her long front legs.

"Nice to meet you both," said Sadie, flashing them a smile, which they reciprocated. "Walli, I can see you've got lovely teeth. You must take very good care of them. And Clifford, although I must apologise because I don't know what kind of creature a platypus is, even though you don't appear to have any teeth your bill is in great shape. Well done."

Walli and Clifford blushed with pride.

"Forget about them. What about me?" interrupted Aubrey very rudely. "I'm the important one."

"You're as ill-mannered as you were the last time I saw you, all those years ago. Even when you were a chick, you were big-headed and bossy," said Sadie in a telling-off voice. "And you don't seem to know your body very well either. Don't you know that, just like Clifford, you don't have teeth? No birds do. So you can't have toothache."

"Then what's the problem?" asked Aubrey, embarrassed about his lack of knowledge of his own beak.

"I think I know, but I need to take a closer look," said Sadie. "I'll be just a minute and this won't hurt a bit." With that she climbed right inside Aubrey's beak, her back legs being the last things to vanish.

The horror-struck look on Aubrey's face made Clifford glance away to stop himself from bursting out laughing.

"You shouldn't eat so many sweets, Aubrey," said Sadie as she crawled around inside his beak examining him.

"How do you know I eat lots?"

"There's bits of chocolate and toffee all over the place in here," she replied, her voice muffled. "It's very unpleasant and I'll need to have a good wash when I'm finished." There was a pause. "And what on Animaux is this? Goodness me, it's a price label for a packet of biscuits. Can't you even wait to unwrap your food before eating it?"

"I was hungry that day. And the biscuits were custard creams – my favourite."

Sadie was quiet for a few minutes. Then she said, "Fixed it" and shortly afterwards she climbed out of Aubrey's beak. "That was a horrible experience for me, Aubrey," she said, looking at him. "Your oral hygiene is generally very poor – you must take much better care of your beak."

"What was the problem?" he asked.

"You had a small crack in your beak on the left-hand side at the back. You were suffering from beak-ache. I've put some filling in the crack. It will take about four hours to set properly, and things should be fine after that. But no eating until then. OK?"

"OK," said a humbled Aubrey. "And I'll be more careful about my beak in the future."

"That's a good turkey," replied Sadie.

Suddenly the most terrible groaning, rumbling noise came from Walli's tummy.

"Oh, I'm terribly sorry," she said, looking embarrassed. "It's just that I'm so hungry."

"Me too," added Clifford. "We haven't eaten all day."

"You poor things," said Sadie. "Tell you what – would you like to stay for dinner? I'm going to cook spaghetti with tomato sauce and I'd be happy to share it with you. You can go home afterwards."

"We'd love to stay," chimed Walli and Clifford, jumping up and down in excitement.

"Would there be a small bowlful for me as well?" asked Aubrey hopefully.

"No, I'm afraid not," said Sadie. "As I just said, you won't be able to eat for another four hours. So I suggest you go home now and as quickly as possible – it's just started to rain."

One hour later Sadie was in the kitchen of her apartment above her dental practice, clearing away the plates and cutlery. Meanwhile Clifford and Walli were sitting at the dinner table in her front room, waiting for her to bring in their dessert of mango pie with fresh whipped cream.

Clifford sighed in contentment and patted his belly. "That was the best spaghetti and tomato sauce I've ever tasted. It was good for my beak."

"I agree," said Walli. "Delicious!"

Clifford thought for a moment. "Do you know what the silly thing about all this is?"

"That, by being selfish, Aubrey came out worst?" answered Walli.

"Well, that's one thing. But what I mean is that Aubs forgot something very important today. And that is that chocolate gives him a really bad headache. Don't you remember two months ago when, without your permission, he took a bite from the bar of chocolate that Martha the Manatee gave you? Well, he had to lie on his bed for about four hours afterwards, the pain was so bad. And then he had to wear sunglasses for the next two days, because the light hurt his eyes."

"Oh yes, you're right. And today he ate much more chocolate than last time. Poor Aubrey!"

"Poor Aubs, my flipper," hissed Clifford. "I wouldn't wish a bad headache on him or any other creature. But perhaps this will finally teach him that he needs to stop being so selfish and unfriendly. We've taken care of him brilliantly recently, especially you, Walli. And yet he's too mean to even give us one of his chocolates as a thank you. He will soon discover that all the chocolate he gorged will come home to roost. That's one of my mum's favourite expressions – and it means that the unpleasant thing that will happen is his fault."

Although Walli felt sorry about what would happen to Aubrey, she nodded in agreement with Clifford.

The platypus continued. "This gives us an opportunity. Since he took our bedroom curtains down, I'm going to take down the ones in his bedroom and hang them in ours. He won't be able to stop me because he won't have the strength to get out of bed. And if he complains afterwards, I'll just say that I'll tell Douglas about his big trick to cheat him out of four silver dollars. Aubs is a coward when you face up to him." Having made his point, Clifford gave another contented sigh and settled further back in his chair. "Life is good, my little warthog friend," he said. "Life is good."

And Walli twinkled back a lovely little smile in agreement.

Meanwhile, a soaking wet Aubrey stumbled back up Fluffy Cloud Lane, his head thumping. The pain caused lights to flash in front of his eyes, even though it was dark. The chocolate made him feel sick. His headache made him feel sick. But what made him feel most sick was his growing realisation of how nasty he had recently been to his good friends. He had to change. He had to learn to be nice. And he would start as soon as his dreadful headache had gone away.

FOUR

THE WEIRD SISTERS

Island of Animaux location:

»   latitude 59° north

»   longitude 5° west

SCENE ONE – AN EVIL PLOT IS HATCHED

All was generally quiet in the little house at the end
of Fluffy Cloud Lane as the sun finally broke through
an enormous bank of haze that had been resting on
Mount Verticus since just before dawn.

Walli and Clifford were in the back garden, trying
– but failing – to catch copperfish in the icy mountain

stream that ran through the garden. They didn't mean
to harm the copperfish; they just wanted to look at
them more closely and see if they could speak. Then
they would throw them back.

Their various attempts to catch the copperfish had
all met with complete failure. First, they had tried using
Aubrey's fishing rod. Then one of the turkey's hairnets,
and finally their trotters and flippers. But the copperfish
had evaded them on every occasion, and they taunted
the warthog and the platypus by swimming around in
circles, blowing triumphant multi-coloured bubbles
and sticking their tails out of the water.

Aubrey was having a mid-morning snooze in his armchair. He was back to his old and rather lazy self, following his adverse reaction to Surgeon Scorpion's sting and his chocolate fancies gluttony. And strangely enough, even though the chocolate had given him a terrible headache, which had taken him three days to recover from, it had also acted as an antidote to the sting. The turkey had confirmed this in a phone call to the scorpion. So Aubrey's madness had subsided, and he had kept his promise to himself and had begun to try to be a better friend to Walli and Clifford.

Down on Wincot High Street, Rick Rat was considering his options. His objective was simple – make that creep Aubrey the Turkey suffer for the stinging nettle fizz incident. Although that had happened five weeks before, the rat was still occasionally emitting foul, eggy burps. He was back to his normal size, not because a needle had been stuck in him at the hospital but because he had suddenly let out the most enormous uncontrolled fart in the waiting room. The force of the fart had propelled Rick from one side of the room to the other, flying over the heads of the other creatures like an out-of-control rocket. And the shockwave from

the fart, along with its terrible smell, had set off the smoke alarm, activated the water sprinkler system, and forced all the creatures in the waiting room to run outside, choking and gasping for breath.

Rick thought he would visit his good friend Harry the Hyena to see if his spotted carnivorous chum had any bright ideas about how the rat could gain his revenge. And so, with bad will his motivation, he pushed open the door of the hyena's replacement intestines dispensary to find Harry behind the counter.

As usual Harry was standing on his hind legs, wearing a soiled apron, a meat cleaver in one paw and a butcher's hook in the other. Rick knew that the dispensary had a mysterious back room, where Harry often went to chop things up. But the rat had never ventured into the room to find out what 'things' were chopped there.

"All right, Harry, how's business?" asked Rick in a matey way, pleased to see his friend again.

"All right, Rick. Nice to see you again. Business? Listen, mate, to tell you the truth, things are a bit slow. The demand for intestines has gone very soft lately, with so many creatures trying to live more healthily. Mate, I'm barely making ends meet these days. My stock doesn't stay fresh long and I've tried many ways to shift it. I've done 80% discounts for senior creatures, 50% off for everyone on Friday afternoons, BOGOF offers. But all have been miserable failures. So I'm considering diversifying into snacks – do you think there's a demand for nail clippings, perhaps from horses or cows?"

"I wouldn't know," said Rick. "Whenever I chew my own nails, I swallow what I bite off. That fills me up. But perhaps you could sell the clippings in bags, and maybe give them different flavours like salt and vinegar or cheese and onion… Creatures might be interested in that, to munch on as they watch television. Of course, my toenails only taste of rat with dirty feet."

"Flavoured nail clippings? Good idea, Rick, I'll look into that. Anyway, what can I do for you today?"

"I need some help, Harry. Aubrey the Turkey is an evil bird and he's also my biggest enemy. I still bitterly regret not eating him when he was an egg. I had a chance once, but his rotten dad got in the way. Anyway, recently Aubrey forced me to drink something he had made. I didn't want to drink it, but he twisted my tail until I had no choice," lied the devious rat, clearly no stranger to inventing fake news. "It was disgusting stuff and it made me very ill. In fact, I had to go to hospital, and Aubrey taunted me when I was there."

"I'm sorry to hear that, Rick," replied Harry sympathetically, quietly noting that the rat's breath had an unpleasant eggy quality to it. "I've always thought that Aubrey was trouble – fancying himself, with his tatty green cardigan and stupid bobble hat, and looking down his beak at the rest of us. So what help do you need?"

"I want something bad to happen to Aubrey. Something that will make it clear to him that I am not a rat to be messed with. Something that will force him to respect me."

"Do you want me to do a job on him? You know, make him 'disappear'?" growled Harry enthusiastically, spotting a chance to increase his stock of intestines.

Rick paused before replying. Harry's offer was tempting, but a cool head was needed when the subject of foul play was in the air.

"That's very kind of you, Harry. But the risk is too high. You are a true professional but there is always the chance of paw prints being left, stray feathers being found, et cetera. Know what I mean? And if there is any evidence left, no matter how small, then we both know the Crow Police will find it. Nothing escapes their beady eyes and they are such great detectives that they will soon realise it was us and come knocking on our doors."

Rick paused again, still clear about what he wanted to happen to Aubrey, but unsure how it could be achieved. "Harry, can you think of any other way that something bad could happen to Aubrey that wouldn't mean another creature being directly involved?"

Familiar with the dark arts, Harry didn't need to think before he gave his reply. "What about the Weird Sisters? Have you thought about visiting them?"

"The Weird Sisters?" replied Rick, a quizzical look on his little cone-shaped, bewhiskered face. "But surely they are just a legend?"

"No, they're real enough," said Harry, seeing an opportunity to present himself as an expert on the subject. "But mate, first let me ask you a really important question. The Weird Sisters will only see creatures that have black hearts. Black hearts are only possessed by creatures who are truly evil. If a creature without a black heart tries to fool the Sisters into thinking he or she does have one, then they will spot this and their vengeance will be truly terrible. Do you have a black heart, Rick?"

Rick gulped. "How do I know if it's black if I can't see it?" he replied nervously.

"You don't need to see it," said Harry. "You can feel it. Is your heart stone cold, Rick? Do you not care about anyone except yourself? Do you quietly chuckle to yourself when you see a creature in distress, then not offer to help them? Those are the signs of a black heart."

"That sounds just like me," replied Rick, swelling with new-found confidence and overjoyed that he understood these previously unimagined characteristics of his circulatory organ.

"Excellent," said Harry, exposing his fearsome sharp teeth in a devilish smile. "I'm sure the Sisters will be happy to meet you. Now, as you may know, they are witches. They can cast terrible spells on creatures – spells from which there is rarely any hope of recovery. I am certain that they will be able to think of a spell that will be bad news for Aubrey the Turkey."

"Fantastic! FANTASTIC! I need to see the Sisters as soon as possible," said Rick, rubbing his front paws together in keen anticipation. "Where can I find them?"

"It's a tricky and dangerous journey to reach their lair," cautioned the hyena. "They live in a cave about halfway up Mount Verticus, on the sea-facing side. So, the opposite side to Aubrey's house. To get there you will need to go all the way across the top of Verticus. You will then see, standing on its own, a blasted oak tree, struck by lightning many years ago. By the side of the tree is the start of a narrow stone path. The path will take you down the mountainside to the entrance of the Weird Sisters' cave. But I must warn you, the path is treacherous. It is steep and slippery, and fierce winds blow all around – many creatures with black hearts that have tried to go down it have lost their footing or been blown off and have plunged to their death on the sharp rocks at the base of Mount Verticus. Also, the path is much more difficult to come up than go down. So don't be lulled into a false sense of security if you think the hardest part is seeing the Sisters."

"That is all clear," said Rick, drinking in Harry's words of advice. "And the Sisters can cast any kind of spell, no matter how dark and awful?"

"Any kind," confirmed Harry, although he was just guessing. He had never seen the Sisters.

"Brilliant! I'll leave right away. Thanks, Harry – I owe you big-time."

"Before you rush off, let me give you a final word of advice. In return for casting a spell, the Sisters will expect to be rewarded. They are particularly fond of precious things, like jewels or gold. Also sardines. So make sure you take something of value with you."

"I'm a bit short of cash at the moment, Harry. Could you lend me a silver dollar?" replied Rick, as usual setting his sights low and thinking that he could somehow negotiate a special offer from the Sisters.

"With pleasure," replied Harry, tossing the coin in the rat's direction. "You can pay me back next Sunday."

Scene Two – The Diabolical Bargain

Rick scurried out of town and up Fluffy Cloud Lane as fast as his little legs could carry him. He stopped briefly outside the gate to Aubrey's front garden to stick out his tongue at the turkey's house. And then he continued his malevolent journey. Rick was soon at the rim of Mount Verticus. He rushed across the broad, flat, grass-covered top, squeaking in excitement at what he was about to do. As he ran, he didn't even notice the wonky, faded lines of the football pitch that the Animaux Cup Final had been played on. And he didn't think about the painful end to his afternoon as referee.

After a lot of scampering and joyful skips, at last he reached the far, sea-facing side. Rick noticed that it had got much colder. He put this down to the fact that it was now evening and the sun had begun to set. Standing in front of him, alone, was the blackened oak tree, just as Harry had told him. Rick approached the tree cautiously, looking around to see if any other creatures were nearby. But, like the oak tree, he was quite alone.

When he got to the tree, Rick sniffed it. He wasn't surprised to find that it smelt of burnt wood. And then he saw the narrow path that started beyond it and snaked away over the rim of Mount Verticus and down into the abyss beyond.

With the light beginning to fade, Rick knew that there was no time to lose. And so, although fearful of what could happen next, the rat walked over to the path and gingerly stepped on it. Then he took a more confident second step. He was on his way, and anxiety caused his heart to thunder in his little chest. At the same time his mouth was bone dry with fear.

Down the steep and slippery path he travelled, towards the cave of the Weird Sisters. He pressed himself into the side of the cliff as he descended, realising this was the safest course of action. But the blustery wind buffeted the rat. Perhaps it was the

wind, or maybe it was some strange supernatural force, but something was pulling Rick away from the safe side of the path to the dangerous, sheer-drop side. If he fell, it would certainly take the rat to his doom.

But no disaster befell him. After what seemed to be an eternity of desperate scrabbling and scrambling, Rick finally reached the cave. A flaming torch burned outside the entrance: fiery rags wrapped around the end of a pole that had been jammed into the rock face. Rick found the light and the tiny amount of warmth that the torch offered strangely comforting.

He didn't pause but went straight into the cave, fearing that another fierce gust of wind might snatch him away at his moment of triumph.

The cave was dark and almost quiet. The only sounds were water, dripping from the ceiling and running down the walls, and a more distant mysterious, bubbling noise. As Rick walked further into the cave, he saw that more fiery torches had been jammed into the rock face, belching dark smoke but giving just enough illumination to light the way.

Rick must have been following a passageway, because he suddenly noticed that he was turning a corner that led to a circular chamber. Yet more torches were burning from the wall and, on the floor in the middle of the chamber, carefully arranged branches were ablaze. Above the fire, suspended on a three-legged frame, was a giant cauldron. Steam was rising from it, hitting the ceiling then rolling along it. Rick couldn't see the cauldron's contents, but it was making the bubbling noise he had noticed earlier.

The rat's eyes were becoming accustomed to the gloom. He spotted three round wicker baskets by the wall, each of which had a blanket on it. On top of the blankets was a selection of soft toys – perhaps playthings, as they were all scratched and chewed. Each basket had a silver tray beside it. And each tray was full of what looked like grey gravel.

To his horror, Rick then spotted three dark figures standing on the opposite side of the cauldron from him. The shock of seeing them made his heartrate increase wildly, and he had to bite his tongue to stop himself screaming in terror.

"All hail Rick Rat," said the three figures simultaneously. "Hail to thee, King of Rodents."

Rick was quite taken aback by these unexpected words, and for a moment he couldn't think of anything to say.

The figures, perhaps not getting the reaction they had expected, huddled together and started whispering, mixed with the occasional purr. Rick could just make out what they were saying.

"Perhaps he's a little deaf. Maybe he didn't hear us."

"I thought you were mumbling a little."

"No, I wasn't!"

"The two of you stop arguing and let's try again!"

The figures turned once again to face Rick.

"All hail Rick Rat," they again said together. "Hail to thee, King of Rodents."

"And I'm pleased to meet you," said Rick, relaxing slightly. "I heard you the first time. There's nothing wrong with my hearing. Sorry I didn't reply – I was just very surprised that you had started to talk."

This answer seemed to satisfy the figures, and they all gave deep purrs of what Rick assumed was approval. Then they began to shuffle in perfect unison in an anti-clockwise direction around the cauldron and towards Rick. This alarmed him slightly. He stepped back, preparing himself for he didn't know what.

The figures somehow seemed to sense his discomfort and spoke to him again as one as they continued to shuffle. "Fear not us three, Rick Rat. Rodent that is black of heart and that wants a bad thing to happen to another creature. Fear not us three."

At last the creatures were in front of Rick. They were three identical black cats, all standing upright on their hind legs. They were wearing black hooded gowns and each had a yellowish-orange bindi spot on their foreheads. Rick wondered if they were triplets.

"So you are the Weird Sisters?" asked Rick, studying the cats as they licked their front paws in purrfect harmony.

"We don't like being called that," they replied. "We much prefer being called the Three Sisters."

"My apologies," said Rick. "No offence meant. Can I ask your names?"

For the first time the cats replied separately.

"My name is Sister," said the first cat.

"And my name is Sister as well," said the second cat.

"And so is mine," said the third cat.

"Well, that's easy to remember," said Rick,

beginning to think that things were starting to become even more peculiar, if that was even possible.

"We know what is in your black heart, Rick," miaowed the cats, again at the same time. "We can read your mind. We know that you want something bad to happen to Aubrey the Turkey, the plump fowl that lives in the little house at the end of Fluffy Cloud Lane. As a special offer, we can also arrange for something bad to happen to his friends, Clifford Platypus and Walli Hogg. Would you like that?"

Rick was tempted to accept the offer, but then he remembered that he only had one silver dollar to pay the Sisters. "No – just Aubrey, thank you. He has been wicked to me, and so now I want something wicked to happen to him."

"Very good," purred the Sisters. "We can make him explode. We can make him grow twelve extra wings. We can cause his head to fall off, sprout little legs and run about on its own."

"I like the sound of all of those things," squeaked Rick, imagining what Aubrey would look like if each happened to him. "I understand you expect to receive a reward for any spells you cast. How much would each of the ones you've just mentioned cost?"

"Nine sardines or your soul," replied the Sisters, staring at him intently. They were clearly business-minded. "Do you have nine sardines with you, Rick?"

"No, I'm fresh out of sardines," came the rat's rather hasty reply.

"Then it will have to be your soul," said the Sisters, beginning to lick their front paws again.

Rick was rather attached to his soul, and wasn't willing to give it up so easily. "Do you have any other spells that cost a bit less?" he asked, wondering how far his silver dollar would stretch.

"For three diamonds, we will turn his feathers bright pink. For three rubies, we will make his toenails grow thirty centimetres long and be impossible to cut. For five gold eagles, we will cause his head to disappear up his bottom."

"They all sound wonderful," said Rick, desperately wishing he had more money. "But they're still too expensive. Do you have anything cheaper?"

The Sisters looked impatiently at him. "How much money have you got?" they miaowed, sounding irritated.

Rick could tell that they were starting to get cross, and desperately hoped that his answer would not offend them further. "I have one silver dollar," he answered nervously, wondering what the consequences of the disclosure would be.

"Is that all?" hissed the Sisters, obviously very annoyed. "If we had known you had so little money, we wouldn't have lit the torches or got the cauldron bubbling! All that toil and trouble – for nothing! We should have given you the economy version of our show. Do you know how much it costs to arrange all these special effects? And have you any idea how much it costs to cast a spell these days? A silver dollar will barely cover our expenses. There will be no profit margin! Cheap rat. Cheap rat. Cheap rat. Thrice cheap rat!"

"I'm s-s-sorry for wasting your time," stammered Rick. "I didn't mean to put you to so much inconvenience. I am only a poor rat and to me one silver dollar is a lot of money."

The Sisters looked at Rick with critical green eyes. Then they once again huddled together and began to whisper. This time Rick couldn't make out what they were saying.

Their conference over, the Sisters turned to face him once more. "Very well, Rick, rodent with a black heart.

We will put a spell on Aubrey. The cost will be one silver dollar – and three of your whiskers. Take it or leave it."

"I'll take it," replied Rick without hesitation, thinking that he would soon be able to regrow his whiskers. "What is the spell?"

"We will make Aubrey the Turkey very sad. More sad than he has ever been before. So sad that he will be crying torrents of bitter tears."

"And will he stay sad for the rest of his life?" asked Rick, eagerly hoping the Sisters would say 'yes'.

"Only one thing can reverse the spell," replied the sisters. "Aubrey will need to soar like an eagle and find his true love."

"Ha ha!" shouted Rick in triumph. "That fat fowl will never fly and there's no chance of him ever being loved by another creature. And so he will stay sad forever. Excellent! Excellent!"

The rat paid the Sisters for the spell. He had hoped they would use sharp scissors to snip off his whiskers, but instead they pulled them out by the roots. This made him scream like a baby and caused his eyes to water.

The Sisters then began to cast their spell, which would be effective immediately, by muttering strange words and making elaborate paw movements.

Rick took this as his cue to leave. Off he scampered towards the cave entrance. As he neared it, he heard a faint cry from the Sisters.

"'Tis done. The turkey will be sad!"

SCENE THREE – WHAT A ROTTEN RAT!

At the mouth of the cave, before he started his journey back up the narrow path, for the second time that day Rick rubbed his little front paws together in glee. "I have Aubrey in my palm – he is hexed! Tomorrow I will visit him, to see his river of tears. And how I will laugh!"

Rick looked from the cave entrance out across the sea. The usual thick mist was in the distance. A full moon was shining down, reflecting off the dark, undulating sea and providing good light. And the wind was no longer gusting. Both of these factors would make it easier for Rick to walk back up the path to the top of Mount Verticus. As he climbed the path, he began to whistle a merry little tune. It was a long time since he had had such a good day. He would sleep well on the pile of rags in his pipe home that night.

Meanwhile, in the little house at the end of Fluffy Cloud Lane Aubrey was still asleep, this time in bed after an uneventful day. He had been dreaming about food and drinks and sweets. And gold and silver.

But suddenly his dream changed. In his new dream, he was sitting in a school classroom many years before. And he was feeling desperately sad. The Sisters' spell had started to take effect! Still fast asleep and with tears streaming down his cheeks, Aubrey tossed uncomfortably in his bed while blurting out a distressed gobble.

Poor, sad Aubrey. But the worst was yet to come.

FIVE

BECAUSE OF ONCE UPON A TIME

_____

Island of Animaux location:

» latitude 40° north

» longitude 73° west

SCENE ONE – GORGEOUS GRUB,
GRIZZLING GOBBLER

"Pass the butter please, Walli," Clifford said as they sat eating breakfast at the kitchen table of the little house at the end of Fluffy Cloud Lane.

"Here you are," replied Walli, carefully pushing the butter plate towards him.

On this lovely, sunny morning the two friends were enjoying a little treat. Martha the Manatee had become concerned that there never seemed to be any food in Aubrey's house – at least, none worth eating – and she worried that Walli and Clifford might become malnourished. Martha didn't worry so much about Aubrey; it was his house, it was his responsibility to look after his guests, and anyway he looked fat enough to survive without food for a few days. And she was hurt that he hadn't thanked her for the baskets of food she had delivered to him when he was ill.

She had started to send Walli and Clifford baskets of food, brought up to the top of Mount Verticus by a huffing, puffing, none-too-happy-about-it Georgina the Goat. This morning the basket had contained a beautiful freshly baked loaf of bread and a packet of butter. And it was this that the friends were enjoying for breakfast.

Clifford settled back in his chair and gave a little sigh of pleasure as he bit into his well-buttered slice of bread – his fourth in under ten minutes. He was beginning to feel a little bit full and his belly was swelling nicely. So just two more slices and the job would be done. It

would also mean that there would be no bread left for Aubrey, and that would be OK in Clifford's book.

Aubrey had not been very friendly that morning. Clifford and Walli had got up at the same time and had come downstairs together. They found Aubrey sitting in his armchair wearing his bobble hat, dressing gown with pyjamas underneath and bunny rabbit slippers, and they had both politely said 'good morning' to him. But he had rudely ignored them, instead choosing to stare with red-rimmed, unblinking eyes toward the window. Aubrey looked really miserable. They thought he must be feeling sorry for himself, although they had no idea why.

But the arrival of the basket of food distracted Clifford and Walli. They were very hungry, so they decided there would be plenty of time later to ask Aubrey what was wrong. Clifford and Walli also felt that they'd need full stomachs to prepare them for listening to Aubrey's latest tale of gloom and woe.

Walli helped herself to another slice of bread. She found the butter hard to spread, as she had trouble holding the knife with her trotters. So, as usual, she put a blob of butter near the edge of the slice. Clifford watched her lift up the slice to take a bite. Walli closed her eyes and opened her mouth. But just before she bit the bread, the butter fell off and landed on the floor. Chewing, Walli mumbled, "Gorgeous", but Clifford noticed a tiny look of surprise on her face, which swiftly morphed into a look of disappointment, as she seemed to realise that the bread hadn't tasted exactly as she had expected.

When they had finished their breakfast the two friends decided to do their good deed for the day.

"Right, let's go and see what's wrong with old misery guts," said Clifford.

They went into the front room. Clifford noticed that Walli had trodden on the missing blob of butter without realising it, and was leaving a little yellow buttery trail behind her as she walked.

They found Aubrey still sitting in his armchair, staring out of the window. He didn't seem to have moved at all.

Walli stopped and looked at him. "What's wrong, Aubrey? You look very unhappy this morning. Can we help?"

This show of concern seemed to break the trance that Aubrey was in. He turned to face Walli, tears in his eyes. "It's nothing, really. It's just that I've suddenly become very sad. It started in a dream last night and I still feel sad today. Perhaps I'll start to feel better later."

Clifford chipped in. "Why are you sad, Aubs? Is it because you've got fleas, or because you smell a bit like unwashed socks?"

"No, it is not, you unpleasant platypus!" gobbled the indignant turkey. "I don't have fleas and I don't smell – do I?" he asked, looking hopefully at Walli.

"No, of course you don't. At least, not today." She turned and faced Clifford. "I think you should say sorry – that wasn't a nice thing to say."

"Why is it always me who needs to apologise?" he quackled back. "I'm not the one sitting there with a face like a wet Sunday afternoon."

Walli glared at him.

"Oh, all right, then." Clifford sighed. "I'm sorry, Aubs. I'm sorry. Now can we find out what's wrong before I get old and my fur turns grey?"

Walli turned back to Aubrey. "Would you like to talk about your problem, Aubrey? We're your friends, and friends help each other when one of them is feeling unhappy."

"Bless you, you are a lovely little warthog," said Aubrey, and for a moment a small smile appeared on his face. "And you are also nice sometimes, Clifford. Sometimes."

"No worries, mate," said Clifford. Had Aubrey just paid him a compliment? "Anyway, what's troubling you? Come on, spit it out."

Aubrey took a deep breath. His face once again became very sad. "Well, it's because of once upon a time. It was a long time ago, when I was at school."

"What happened?" asked Walli. "Did you get a bad mark from one of your teachers? Were you naughty in the playground? Did you come last in a race on sports day?"

Aubrey, clearly deep in thought, waited a few seconds before answering. "No, it was none of those things." He took a deep breath. "The truth is, I fell in love."

"In love? Is that all?" groaned Clifford, perhaps disappointed that it wasn't something much more unpleasant and embarrassing. "But why has that made you so miserable? I thought being in love was supposed to make you happy. Everyone I've seen who has been in love has the same silly, dreamy look on their face. And all they want to do is smell flowers. Sorry to mention it, but they are just like you were on the night that Claudette was supposed to visit. Very strange indeed."

Aubrey scowled at Clifford. He was still deeply upset by the tragic ending met by his crane fly love. "You are only a simple platypus. Love is a complex thing. You wouldn't understand it."

"Well, educate me, Casanova. Let's see if you can teach me something," replied Clifford.

"Aubrey, what was her name?" asked Walli. "By the way, I think of poor Claudette every day. I'm so sorry for what happened."

Aubrey nodded an acknowledgement at Walli's latest apology. Tears welled in his eyes as he answered her question. "Beatrice. She joined my class in our last year in school and she used to sit at a desk across the classroom from me. She was quite beautiful and she had a lovely smile."

"And did you talk to her, perhaps at break time?" continued Walli.

"Oh, we never spoke," replied Aubrey.

This surprised Clifford and Walli.

"Never spoke? Then how can you say you were in love with her?" gasped the platypus.

"I just knew I was. And she really loved me," said Aubrey.

"But how do you know, if you never talked to each other?" asked Walli in a concerned voice.

"Just from the way she looked at me. When our eyes met, she smiled. And she sent me a Valentine's Day card. I found it on my desk when I came in one morning."

"How do you know it was from her?" replied Walli.

"Well, it was signed from 'a secret admirer' but for the rest of that day I noticed that she kept looking at me, shyly smiling every time. I think she was hoping that I would notice and talk to her."

"And so why didn't you?" said Walli, starting to feel as sad as Aubrey.

"Because I was playing it cool. Because I was playing hard to get. But it was actually impossible to get," answered the turkey quietly, shaking his head in despair. "It's only now that I realise how stupid I was. She was lovely, but for the rest of the year I just ignored her. She began to look quite sad, and when the year was over I left school and never saw her again."

"That's awful," squealed Walli, feeling very emotional. A few tears started to appear in the corners of her beautiful little black eyes.

"I know! I know!" whimpered Aubrey, looking at his slippers and feeling worse than ever. "All I can do is think how silly I was. I wish I'd behaved differently and been nicer to her. I wonder what she's doing now. I suppose I'll never know. I'll never know…"

Clifford returned to the conversation. "I feel really sorry for you, mate. But there is one thing I've got to know. Aubs – was Beatrice a crane fly? I only ask because you know how surprised I was when you told me about Claudette…"

"No, of course she wasn't," replied Aubrey crossly.

"Well, was she some other kind of odd creature?" pressed the platypus. "You know, the type that makes the fur on the back of your neck – or, in your case, feathers – stand up when you think about it? Like a slug or a bug or a creepy-crawly?"

"Absolutely not!" gobbled Aubrey, getting even more angry with Clifford. "Why would you ask such a question? Can't you see how upset I am?"

"Sorry, Aubs," said Clifford, realising that he had been a little too nosey and holding up his flippers in defence. "I didn't mean to get you worked up. I was just curious. So Beatrice was a turkey, right?"

"I don't know what gave you that idea. If you must know, she was a bee. But not just any kind of bee. She was a Queen Bee. Actually, she was a Princess Bee then, but she'll have grown into a real Queen by now. She was my beauty queen."

Clifford's bill fell open in amazement. "Aubs, you never cease to amaze me. Look mate, you left school ages ago. Aren't you putting Beatrice on a pedestal? I mean, are you remembering her correctly? Perhaps she wasn't as nice as you think."

Aubrey glared at him. "How dare you, Clifford? You weren't there. You don't know how much I cared for her."

This made the platypus realise how deep Aubrey's feelings were. And so there was only one solution he could suggest. "If you still feel like this about Beatrice all these years later, there's only one thing to do."

"What's that?" asked Aubrey.

"You need to find her and talk to her. To sort things out. But you'd better do it sooner rather than later – it's the only way to stop yourself from feeling miserable."

"Do you know where she lives, Aubrey?" asked Walli.

"I'm not sure where she lives now, but she used to live in a beehive on top of Black Rock. That's near Arenas Junction, in the middle of the Great Plunder Plain."

"Black Rock sounds like an interesting place. How do you get there?" asked Clifford.

"By train, from Wincot to Arenas Junction. Then it's a two-hour walk across the Great Plunder Plain – and you need to watch out for the acid-spitting scarab beetles, the screaming hairy trotter-splitters, the nose-less magnetic beak-grabbers, the invisible stinking mini bogs, the petrified razor-sharp tree stumps and the scorching quicksand."

"I'm not sure it sounds like a very nice place," said Walli. "I'm worried the screaming hairy trotter-splitters might be interested in my dainty little feet."

"You'll be fine, my hairy friend. I'll protect you," quackled Clifford. "It sounds like great fun, and I suggest we leave straight away for Wincot railway station. Aubs, we'll come with you and you can pay for our tickets."

Aubrey thought for a while. "I'm not sure, Clifford. What would I say to Beatrice if I met her? What if she doesn't remember me? Perhaps it's best that we forget about the whole thing."

Walli spoke firmly, putting her fear about the trotter-splitters to one side. "Aubrey, you're starting to make excuses. There's only one way to deal with this problem and that is to face it. You know in your heart that's true."

Aubrey knew that his friends were correct. Tears suddenly flowed down his cheeks. "Walli, whatever would I do without you?" he blubbed. "You are always so sensible. As are you, Clifford, when you're not saying rude things about me."

Clifford smiled back.

"All right, let's get this over with," said Aubrey, wiping his tears away. Rising from his armchair and taking off his bobble hat, dressing gown and pyjamas, then kicking off his slippers, Aubrey picked up his purse, which lay on the small table beside the armchair. He looked inside it to check there was enough money to buy all their train tickets. There was, just.

Clifford looked at him. "Aren't you going to wear your cardigan? You look quite naked without it."

"I won't need it today," replied the turkey mysteriously. "Come on, let's get going. We need to get to Black Rock before it gets dark."

The three friends started to walk towards the front door.

"Aubs, why is it called Black Rock?"

"The clue is in the name, Clifford. It's because of its colour. It's one hundred metres high, and has smooth dark granite sides all around. No one has ever climbed it before because there's nothing to grip on to. Even Georgina the Goat can't do it, and she's half mountain goat. Although I suspect it's because she is also a quarter billy goat and a quarter silly old goat."

"Well, if Georgina can't make it to the top, then what chance have we got?" asked Walli.

"Don't you worry, we'll be OK," replied Aubrey, and gave her a little wink. "But we will need the basket that Georgina delivered the bread and butter in earlier this morning."

It was standing on the floor by the front door, ready for the goat to collect later, so Clifford picked it up as they went past. They were soon heading down Fluffy Cloud Lane towards Wincot and the railway station. By leaving when they did, they missed Rick Rat's arrival at the house one hour later. The evil rat had hoped to see Aubrey in a distressed state. He muttered in annoyance when nobody opened the door, and reluctantly trudged back to town.

SCENE TWO – THE PLAIN REVEALS ITS SECRETS

After a short wait at the railway station, followed by an uneventful, not including Aubrey's frequent tears, five-hour train ride on the antiquated, bumpy Animaux Railways steam puffer service, the friends arrived at Arenas Junction. No other creatures had been on the train, except the driver and the guard Sara Squirrel, who checked their tickets frequently, each time unhygienically franking them with her teeth.

The friends alighted onto the weed-covered wooden platform. Most trains passed Arenas Junction without stopping, since there was nothing interesting to stop for.

The friends walked off the platform as the steam puffer started to chug back to Wincot. There was only one service each day, so the puffer wouldn't return until the same time tomorrow.

The Great Plunder Plain stretched out in front of them as far as the eye could see. It looked quite desolate, with just a few small bushes and one or two

dead trees, their leafless branches jutting into the sky. A dark thundercloud dominated the horizon, seemingly fixed in position, and a wind gusted, causing dust storms and tumbleweed to blow across the Plain.

The three friends started their long walk towards Black Rock. Aubrey led the way, with Clifford at the rear and Walli in the middle, glancing around nervously for any sign of the trotter-splitters or the other terrible things that Aubrey had mentioned.

After they had walked two kilometres in silence, Clifford stopped. The others stopped too, turned and looked at him.

"What's wrong, Clifford?" asked Walli. "Do you need a rest?"

"I hope not," said Aubrey impatiently. "We've only just started and there's still a long way to go."

"Can't you hear it – and feel it?" asked Clifford, a puzzled look on his face. "Can you hear that low humming sound? It feels like the ground is vibrating."

"You're right, Clifford. I hadn't noticed it because I've been worried about one of the awful creatures Aubrey mentioned suddenly appearing. Aubrey, do you know what's causing the humming and shaking?"

"Oh yes. I forgot to say earlier. As well as all the other terrors I mentioned, apparently there's a huge nest somewhere underneath the Plain, full of gigantic, bad-tempered fire ants. I suppose that's what we can hear and feel. I suggest we keep moving, in case we're close to the entrance."

Without another word the friends set off again, now at a far quicker pace. But much to their relief, the rest of the journey passed without incident, and after two hours the friends had arrived at the bottom of Black Rock. It towered above them, as black and smooth-sided as Aubrey had indicated.

"There's no way we can reach the top," said Clifford, looking up, his flippers resting on his hips. "This has been a wasted journey."

"Not at all," said Aubrey. "This is a chance for me to show you what turkeys do best."

"And what would that be?" asked Clifford. "Make nasty smells, pull silly faces, eat all the food?"

"Of course not," said Aubrey, looking surprised that this was what Clifford thought about him. "What turkeys do best is fly."

Clifford and Walli stared at him in amazement. Had he really just said what they thought?

"Fly?" said Walli. "I didn't know you could fly."

"All turkeys can fly," said Aubrey. "At least, wild turkeys can, and I'm definitely very wild. Look how long I've let my feathers and toenails grow!"

"When did you last fly?" asked Clifford suspiciously. "I only ask because your feathers are a little tatty. Look, there are holes here, and there. Also, you seem to be carrying a bit more weight than is good for you, which will make it difficult for you to take off."

"Actually, I've never flown before. Although that's just because I haven't tried. But it should be easy, especially for a clever bird like me. Taking off may be a little bit of a problem, but if I climb up that petrified tree stump over there and jump off, I should be able to get airborne if I flap my wings hard enough."

Aubrey walked over to the stump. After a bit of a struggle – during which he showed far too much of his bottom to Clifford and Walli – he managed to climb onto it. He stood looking down at them.

"Aubrey," said Walli, "you may be able to fly to the top of Black Rock, but what about us? We can't fly."

"That's why we brought the basket. If you two sit in it, I can hold the handle with my feet and you'll get a free ride."

Clifford had doubts. "I'm not too keen to be close to your feet. I reckon they will smell cheesy. Tell you what, Aubs, why don't you fly to the top of Black Rock and see Beatrice? We'll wait here and we can go back to Wincot together when you're finished."

"Yes. That's a good idea," agreed Walli quickly, secretly pleased that she didn't need to go flying.

"Suit yourselves, yellow-bellies," gobbled Aubrey rudely. "It would serve you right if I decided to fly all the way back to Wincot and leave—"

But before Aubrey could finish his sentence, a terrible shrieking filled the air. The friends looked around, but they couldn't see where it was coming from. But it sounded close, and with every second it was getting much louder, as if whatever was shrieking was rushing toward them. Suddenly about ten screaming creatures, all dribbling furiously and clawing at the air with their sharp talons, appeared in front of them – apparently from out of nowhere, but actually from an invisible stinking bog. Clifford and Wally had assumed the nasty smell from the bog was coming from Aubrey, so they hadn't paid much attention to it.

The creatures rushed forward. They seemed to be making for Walli.

"What are they?" shouted Clifford.

"They're hairy trotter-splitters!" Aubrey gasped. "Quick! Get up here and bring the basket with you. There's no time to lose."

The platypus and the warthog moved more quickly than greased lightning. In an instant they were on the tree stump next to Aubrey, then they leapt in the basket.

"Let's keep our wings, flippers and trotters crossed for luck," said Aubrey, gripping the handle of the basket with his feet. The next moment, he jumped off the tree stump, the basket hanging below him.

For a few milliseconds the friends plummeted towards the ground – and the waiting, very excited hairy trotter-splitters.

Clifford looked up. "Flap your wings, Aubs, flap your wings. Now!" he shouted.

"Sorry, forgot!" replied Aubrey.

Almost immediately, Walli and Clifford felt themselves rising quickly into the air, far from the reach of the trotter-splitters. Above them Aubrey's wings were outstretched and flapping in perfect harmony.

"I can fly, I can fly!" he shouted. "Although it's a bit harder than I thought it would be, and you're very heavy."

Walli took offence. "I'm not heavy, Aubrey. I'm only small and there's not much of me."

"Don't talk, Aubs," advised Clifford. "Save your breath and your strength. You'll need them to reach the top of Black Rock."

Clifford and Walli settled down in the basket and actually began to enjoy the ride – at least, as much as they could with the basket swinging wildly and with Aubrey's bottom being far too close for comfort.

Swoosh went Aubrey's wings above them. Then …
prrrpp.

"What's that?" asked Walli.

But before Clifford could answer, a horrible eggy
smell filled their nostrils.

"He's farting," choked Clifford. "It's because of the
effort he's putting into flying. It's revolting, but we'll
just have to put up with it. Look – it's not too much
further to the top of Black Rock. But what a stink!"

And so the flight continued.

Swoosh – prrrpp – "Urgh!" *Swoosh – prrrpp –*
"Strewth!"

Scene Three – Good Day at Black Rock

At last the top of Black Rock appeared. In the centre of it stood an enormous white beehive. One swarm of bees had just arrived back, full of nectar and pollen from their visit to all the beautiful flowers on Animaux. Another swarm was just leaving, heading for more flowers. It was the bees in this beehive that made all the honey for the island.

"Can't go any further … am exhausted," gasped Aubrey when the friends were fifteen metres from the beehive and about three metres from the ground. He stopped flapping his wings, and the three friends tumbled to the ground. Luckily, none of them were hurt.

"Well done, Aubs," said Clifford as he climbed out of the basket and staggered to his feet.

"Oh, it was nothing," said Aubrey modestly, sitting on the ground, secretly fiercely proud of what he had just done.

A drone bee had watched the arrival of the three friends with great interest. It flew over to them.

"Hello, strangerzzzz," it buzzed. "We don't get many visitorzzzz here. Can I help you?"

"I hope so," replied Aubrey. "I've come to see Beatrice. I think she may be your Queen? Is she at home?"

"Yezzzz, she'zzzz at home, and yezzzz, she'zzzz my Queen. I'll go and tell her you're here. What'zzzz your name?"

"Aubrey," replied the turkey.

"Aubzzzzee," repeated the drone. "Back in a minute." And it buzzed off.

Aubrey waited nervously. His beak felt very dry. Walli and Clifford stood by his side, giving him moral support by gently touching his aching wings.

Suddenly a stunningly beautiful bee emerged from the hive, flew over to Aubrey and landed on the ground in front of him. The bee was much larger than the drone and had superb black-and-yellow diagonal stripes on its abdomen, with wonderful translucent-veined wings folded together on top.

Aubrey recognised Beatrice immediately, and she seemed to recognise him. Both smiled – the widest, happiest smiles you could ever wish to see. Then Aubrey walked a few paces forward to her and, ever so gently, held Beatrice's front legs with his wings. For a moment they stood and looked at each other.

"Hello, Beatrice," he said. His nerves, also his terrible sadness, had vanished the moment he saw her. "It's lovely to see you again. It's been a long time."

"Yezz it hazz, Aubrey," she replied, making a happy buzzing noise. "And it'zz great to zzee you too."

"Beatrice, I had to see you one more time, because there's something I've always wanted to say to you."

"What izz that?" Beatrice asked, the sunlight giving her compound eyes a warm, golden glow.

For only the second time in his life – the first time being during his confrontation with his sister Audrey many months before – Aubrey spoke the truth, straight from his heart. He spoke carefully and clearly, meaning every word he said.

"This is very important to me, Beatrice. I wanted to say that I'm sorry. I'm sorry for not being nice to you at school. For not talking to you, and for not being your friend. I'm sorry I made you unhappy and I'm sorry you stopped smiling at me. I really wish I had been kinder. I realise it's too late to change anything now, and we have our own lives to live. But I am sorry, Beatrice, I truly am." Aubrey held his breath. He wasn't sure how Beatrice would react. Would she be angry? Would she think he had gone crazy? Would she laugh at him and think him a silly old turkey?

But Aubrey needn't have worried. Beatrice gave him the loveliest smile he had ever seen. It caused his tummy to flutter.

"Aubrey, that'zz a lovely thing to zzay. Thank you. It'zz true that I was zzad at zzchool. I thought I had done zzomething to upzzet you. Or that you didn't think I wazz very pretty."

"Beatrice, you didn't do anything wrong. It was me that wasn't nice. I did think you were beautiful. And you still are."

Beatrice blushed. "Thank you, Aubrey. It meanzz zzo much to me. And I alwayzz thought that you were wonderful – definitely the mozzt handzzome creature in the zzchool."

It was Aubrey's turn to blush. "I wonder if we could keep in touch?" he asked. "Perhaps we could send each other letters and phone each other from time to time?"

"I would like that very much," she replied with a warm smile.

"And so would I," said a very happy Aubrey, giving a little hop in celebration.

Beatrice looked at Walli and Clifford. "I'm happy that you've brought your friendzz to keep you company. Later on I'll introduce you to zzome more of my children. You've already met Dariuzz Drone. And if you like, you can zztay to tea. We're having honey – and for you I'll get out zzome of my zzpecial rezzerve, the one with a hint of orange blozzom and elderflower."

"That would be lovely," said Aubrey, unable to take his eyes off her. "Is that OK with you guys?" he said to Walli and Clifford, still looking at Beatrice.

"Yes, absolutely!" they said excitedly.

129

Even the sun seemed to be celebrating the special moment. It shimmered on the horizon as it slowly began to set over the Island of Animaux.

Happy, happy Aubrey the Turkey. The Weird Sisters' spell had been lifted! He would always remember today with great joy.

On that golden evening, as Aubrey basked in the sun's warm rays, which burst through the haze that surrounded the island, revelling in his love for Beatrice and his friends, he never imagined that his time on Animaux would soon come to an end...

THE END

COMING SOON

Aubrey, Clifford and Walli will be back soon with more adventures. Please keep your eyes open for 'Coffee and Ice Cream' and four other tales. For the latest news, continue to check out milomcgivern.com.